喚醒你的英文語感！

Get a Feel for English !

喚醒你的英文語感！

Get a Feel for English !

MP3
走到哪聽到哪

- 8大聽力盲點各個擊破！
- 嚴選11類聽力測驗必考題材！
- 各種情境都能聽懂語意，溝通零失誤！

「系統化」練出好聽力！

陳超明教授帶你聽出語意重點，

改變一生的英文聽力課

作者：政大 **陳超明** 教授

整理：黃郁雯

Listening

Vocab

Reading

貝塔語言出版
Beta Multimedia Publishing

IRT語言測驗中心
Language Testing Center

一、聽力訓練為溝通的第一步

英語溝通從聽懂別人的話開始，聽力訓練逐成為溝通學習的第一步。傳統的聽力訓練，要求學習者不斷地聽，熟悉各種聲調或發音的規則，缺乏專業的技巧訓練與自學的方法。這本書希望提供基本與進階的技巧訓練，並期望學習者能有自我練習的方式。

二、本書的特點：如何突破聽力障礙

一般非母語人士對於聽懂別人的英語，其障礙大概有兩層：一是對於某些單字不熟悉，甚至有些單字似曾聽過或學過，但一時無法與語意聯結；二是對於整體語意抓不到重點，無法在腦子中形成溝通所需要的訊息。本書即針對這兩個障礙提出解決的學習技巧。從聯結聲音與語意開始，練習聽力者必須自我複誦，將聽講結合；此外，指出各種英文句子必須知道的重點，並導入各種情境，讓學習者能輕鬆聽懂，且能抓住重點。

針對這些障礙，我們提供了訓練聽力的技巧篇，強調口語複誦的重要性，學習者一定要依照書中的指示，說出或複誦所聽到的英文，這樣才能將聲音與語意結合。音調、連音、語氣、斷句的練習更能強化對於英語這種有節奏語言的熟悉度。

情境練習篇不僅提供各種情況所碰到的英語，更從單字與表達方式，提供學習者更深入的練習機會。學習者在真實生活情境中，即可馬上進入狀況。

三、如何使用本書

本書主要是針對學生及社會人士，在真實生活中所面臨的英語情境，加以分類及整理，提供完整的聽力練習空間。所有的情境英語都是從真實環境中截取下來，非教科書中的英語。從電視新聞氣象到學術演講，提供有效且實用的練習機會。掌握聲音及重點，就能在國際溝通場合中，理解對方的語意。更進一步透過複誦，也能加強口語能力。

延續《改變一生系列》的書籍，本書從技巧篇到情境篇，都列出技巧內容、範例與作業，學習者以「做中學」的概念，加強自我聽力的敏感度。

使用本書，首先將技巧篇的所有單元有系統地、一步一步練習，並多次播放本書的聲音光碟。如果剛開始，無法整句聽懂，也可以透過播放器，一個字或兩個字來播放，先熟悉單字的聲音，然後再掌握句子的斷句規則與語調，這樣就可以慢慢聽懂整句話。

做完技巧篇的練習，進入情境篇學習，可以針對現在所面對的工作或生活環境開始練習，不一定需要依照本書的單元次序。將書中的單元情境與現今生活與工作情境結合，更能體會這種真實英語的實用性與即時性。

四、持續練習：上網練實力

語言學習絕對需要持續練習。本書提供一個學習的策略，可以訂定三個月或半年的期間，將本書所有單元練習完後，開始上網到國外的新聞網站、影音網站或教育網站（如 Itune University, TED 等），維持聽英語的習慣。本書也將試題篇（包含 TOEIC 及全民英檢的演練試題）置於「貝塔英語知識館」(http://www.anglepedia.com/beta)，提供題目、音檔、以及詳細解析的線上下載。請讀者在完成本書練習後，進一步上網作測驗。透過不斷地接收英語訊息，相信在國際溝通場合上，可以馬上應用這些實境生活的聽講能力！

政大英文系教授　陳超明

CONTENTS 目錄

英文**聽力訓練**的成功關鍵

聽力訓練的困難

　　聽力訓練面臨的首要問題就是要聽得懂對方在說些什麼。一般來說，要聽得懂對方在說些什麼會遭遇到的困難有：

一、將語音轉換成語意，聽到後馬上就能瞭解訊息。

二、單字辨識力造成的單字停留。

　　有時候聽到一段話，會被其中一個單字困住，困住的狀況不是因為全然不懂這個單字，而是那種似懂非懂、明明很熟悉常聽到卻會意不過來的掙扎，然後就一直陷在非想出那個單字意思不可的掙扎裡而分心，導致忽略了後續的話語內容。這種情形，也常是參加 TOEIC 和 TOFEL 聽力測驗時，失分的致命傷。所以要奉勸大家，不要執著在解讀某個單字的字意上，只要從上下文大概猜測瞭解到單字的意義就好。

三、句型的問題。

　　這層面又包含三個小課題：

1. 單字的語意：如何在短短幾秒內將單字的語音與腦子裡的單字比對轉成字意。

2. 找出語法結構中的重點在哪裡：即聽到時，迅速抓出關鍵字，略過與語意無關的單字。一般而言，非小說敘述且純為平常溝通用的口語，句中結構重點大都會落在動詞與名詞上，即所謂的 content words（有內容的字眼）其它如副詞、形容詞等都不重要，因為它們不會影響語意。

3. 「語調」的問題：英文有輕重之別，說話時的抑揚頓挫會影響到語意，相對地也會影響到聽話者對語意的接收。個人腔調並不會造成對方聽不懂，但是重音下錯位置就會有錯誤判讀和誤解語意的情形發生。

解決之道：進行聽力訓練

解決聽力問題最直接的方式，就是針對幾個要點各個擊破，以下將針對如何進行聽力訓練分別加以說明。

一. 抓出主詞和動詞：

聽英文句子時最重要的就是抓出主詞和動詞。

一般而言，主詞大概分為二種，一個是名詞的人或物，一個是抽象的概念。在口語溝通中，以抽象的概念作為主詞的情況較少，比如說像用 Happiness、Love 這類的字眼當主詞的句子並不會太多，通常會出現的，多是以人稱代名詞如：I、We、He、She、You、They 等作為主詞的句子。

動詞大都跟在主詞之後用來表示一種動作，亦即有內容的字眼。不管是聽廣播、看新聞、脫口秀、……任何類型的講稿，最重要的就是要抓出 strong words，有內容含意的字，其它如語助詞或介詞 in、on、at 就直接讓它過去。以下面這句話為例：

In February, U.S. President Barack Obama approved a bold plan to improve the U.S. economy.

在上列句子中，只要抓出名詞 February、President Barack Obama、plan 與 U.S. economy，及動詞 approved 和 improve，就可以知道整個句子要表達的意思，其它字彙即使沒聽清楚或不懂字意也無所謂。

這是對於聽力不好的人做的初步訓練而言，只要能聽出**名詞**和**動詞**就好。但是，在整個英文的學習過程中，就不建議採這樣的方式，最好能字字都 catch。

二. 提升英文單字的熟悉度

　　聽對方說話時，首要的就是聽出句子中具名詞詞性和動詞詞性的英文單字；再者就是瞬間將單字的聲音轉換成語意。這二點都得藉由平常的練習來增進。可以應用以下三個聽力練習步驟來幫助記憶單字。

Step 1

從自己身邊周遭會遇到或常用的單字開始記，不要用背的概念記單字，用自己的聲音把字念出來，大聲念個五遍錄下來，平常就放給自己聽，用熟悉單字聲音的方式來記單字。聲音記憶最簡單的方法就是善用手邊的工具，如手機或 MP3，隨時隨地將遇到的單字的聲音記錄下來，再反覆播放出來聽以增加印象。總之，**記單字一定要用聲音的方式**。

Step 2

為每個單字造一個句子。這個句子不見得要自己造，你可以上網到國外的 Yahoo 或 Google 網站輸入那個單字，再從搜尋結果中，找一個新聞句子或好句子抄下來，同樣的，不是抄下來背，而是抄下來不斷地複誦，將聲音輸入腦中來強迫記憶。所有的英文學習，不論是句子或單字，都要用聲音來記，訓練自己一聽到發音就能立即轉換成語意。

　　現今，國外的中高階主管或 CEO 很流行做 Voice Memo，就是將自己的交辦事項透過錄音筆或手機錄下來，這也可以用來做為大家學習英文聽力的方式，即時將遇到的單字錄下來後，利用空檔放給自己聽，久而久之，自能練成聽音辨意的功力。

Step 3

瞭解口語英文或新聞報導中常見的英文表達方式與句型結構。基本上，在新聞英語裡頭，它的表達方式和結構是習慣將 Main Idea 放在第二句或第一段最末句裡，不會一開始就進入主題。經典的句型用法，通常會在一開場引用名言佳句、一首詩，或一句幽默的話語來攫取聽眾或觀眾的注意力。

特殊的英文表達

　　接著要談的是特殊的表達方式。這個部分會牽扯到東西方根深蒂固不同的習慣表達方式，大概可分為方向、數字、電話號碼、時間等幾個項目，全是在口語時最容易造成大家在聽力接收上的阻礙點。

方向

中文是採東西定位，英文是採南北定位。如西北航空公司的英文就是 Northwest Airlines 而非 Westnorth Airlines。

數字

中文是採萬定位，英文是採千、百萬來定位。因為英文沒有萬這個單位，而是用 10 千來表示，對於習慣用萬來表示的國人，很容易造成換算表達時的困擾。我建議大家有空時可以常常自我練習，用英文從 1 數到 1,000。此外，出國時，可以將可能會用到的數字先在字卡上做註記隨身攜帶，註記方式要用 45,000（45 thousand）和 2,100（21 hundred）的方式表示。

電話號碼

除了區域號碼，台灣的是八位數，所以我們習慣採 4 個字 4 個字斷句。但美國的電話號碼是 7 位數，所以會採 3 位 4 位來斷。

這邊再補充一下，數字上，最主要是得習慣外國人的斷法或念法，例如住飯店時的房間號碼 1205，正確的念法是 twelve o five，不是中文習慣的

one two zero five 的方式；911 就會念成 nine eleven（而意指緊急電話時，則會唸成 nine one one）。年份 1980 會念成 nineteen eighty，凡是遇到 4 位數就自動兩兩切割來念。

時間

要顛覆以往從教科書學習到的說法，例如 4 點 58 分就直接說 four fifty-eight，不要用 two to five 那種畫蛇添足的說法，一般人通常不會這樣使用。另外，在口語用法上，會先講大的時間單位再提小的時間單位，例如 Let's meet on Sunday. Will 2:45 be okay? 與英文書寫時恰好相反。

　　要克服這些特殊英文表達障礙，除了牢記上述的要點之外，最好的方式就是直接聽母語人士如何表達，多看電視與電影。

成功的關鍵：複誦

英文聽力成功的關鍵就在於「複誦」與「熟悉動詞用法」。

聽力成功的關鍵就是要「複誦」。其實要聽懂意思很簡單，只要習慣聲音語調並掌握住動詞和名詞就可以，但，要想訓練自己擁有與母語人士同等的聽力，一定要下功夫做複誦的動作。

不論是與外國人對話或是聽廣播看各類節目，都要有鸚鵡學舌的精神，在心中默唸或用嘴巴唸出聲，將別人說的句子複誦一遍，而且，要學習到最正確的 Spoken English 最好的方式正是直接模仿學習外國人的說話方式與語調，外國人怎麼講，你就跟著怎麼說，包準不會錯。

要學好聽力，複誦是絕對不可省略的步驟。剛開始進行複誦時，難免會有來不及的問題，不需要擔心，只要將聽到的新聞廣播錄下來，一句一句、一段一段切割，重複聽並跟著複誦，甚至是聽寫下來。每天至少花個十分鐘做這樣的訓練，半年之後，要聽懂一場全英文的演講絕對沒問題。而且，經由如此的訓練，你會發現，你並不只是利用句中的動詞和名詞在猜詞意，而是真的能每字每句都聽懂，即使是冠詞也不會遺漏；在訓練過程中，還能自然熟悉英文口語句型結構與慣用語；當然，也能利用聲音記憶自然而然增進字彙量。

另一個關鍵則是，熟悉動詞的用法。針對場合分別熟記那些場合會出現的動詞群組，如開會時、看新聞時、談話時……諸如此類的。

在聽力上還會遭遇到的難題就是速度和斷句。速度會隨著練習時間的累積而自然進步，斷句只要掌握「一個長句子或一整個段落，通常斷句處會落在動詞或很長的主詞之後」的原則也不難突破。只要大家能把握住上述重點並加以持續不斷的練習，要聽懂英文易如反掌。

口語新聞聽力訓練

一般英文聽力的對象，除了與老外面對面溝通外，最重要的場景就是聽懂新聞報導，如 CNN 新聞。很多人把聽懂新聞英語當作聽力訓練的重要學習指標。新聞英語其實與一般口語英文略有不同。新聞英語的媒介分為二種，一種是報紙，一種是廣播，二種的敘述法有些許不同。

一、句型

在報紙新聞方面，有些專屬的特殊句型，比如說「發言人引述某某人的話」這種特殊用語，又或是將最具震撼力的話擺在第一句，各種句型不定，會依新聞性做選擇使用。但，廣播新聞或電視新聞則不會出現這樣的句型。廣播或電視類的新聞報導，播報方式一定是將新聞主題放在第一個句子中直接講述出來。

口語新聞中的句型結構很簡單，最常見的就是 [S + V + O]，聽的時候只要能抓出主詞、動詞、受詞和數字，句意應該就全部出來了。

二、連音

一般人在聽力上遭遇困難時，通常會直接聯想到的問題就是所謂的「連音」。其實講英文時會遇到的連音字並不多，一般會直接滑過的連音字都是我們稱為弱動詞、弱字的字眼，例如 aren't。

在聽力上常會造成非英語系母語人士混淆的一個發音字就是 can't，因為 t 的音很容易被忽略，所以很難去辨識。在這邊教大家一個最簡單的方法，就是，如果你聽到的 can 是發重音的，八九不離十，應該就是 can't，否定的意思。

三、斷句

事實上，英文聽得慢或聽不懂的主要原因並非連音，而是在於對英文斷句的聲音效果不熟悉，對英文節奏無法掌握。如果能清楚聽到斷句處，就能很順利地一路跟著說話者聽下去。

練習聽斷句時，需一段一段重複聽，自然可聽出英文的韻律與節奏，辨識出斷句處，尤其在音調上揚處要特別注意，語調上揚之後通常都會是斷句的地方。

四、濃縮句型

每則英文新聞播報的時間大概只有 30 秒，要在 30 秒內完全講完一件事，一定得使用最精簡的字數完成。所以，自然會發展出一套濃縮過的專用句型與簡短的專用替代型動詞字彙，這亦是 CNN 與 BBC 英文廣播最大的特色。

廣播與電視新聞，最常使用的口語句型是 [S + V, Ving/Ved]，前面用來述說先發生的事件，後面則是接著發生的事。這種句型的實用性在於，可以省略一個主詞的重複用字，有助於爭取時間的濃縮性。時間的掌握在口語新聞上有絕對的重要性。

五、替代動詞

爭取時間的另一個關鍵就是利用較簡短的字彙來取代一般常用的字彙，讓播報者在播報時能夠更快講完，例如一般會用 destroy 來講「破壞」這個意思，或用 tear apart 講「撕裂」，但，到了口語新聞時，可能就會以

rip 這個字來取代前述二個字的意思，此外，如用 backs up 取代 supports 來縮減念時的音節，用 maker 來取代較長的 manufacturer 這個字等。曾有學者上 CNN 網站，將這類常用替代動詞整理出來，一共歸納出了 70 個新聞常用動詞，只要熟記這些動詞，在聽新聞英語上絕對會有很大的幫助。

此外，像是 wind up 這樣的俚俗語，也是口語英文新聞裡常會用到，報紙新聞卻不會去使用的詞彙。

整體而言，口語英文新聞有其特性，聽英文新聞的時候要跟得上它的音調與節奏。我們一般講話的速度不會那麼快，但是口語新聞為了在時間內播報完，速度會比正常交談時快很多。

在電視英文新聞裡頭，有些典型的句子是常常可以聽到的，例如 "What you are seeing in the video right now ..."，因為電視新聞都會有影片畫面，所以這個句子就會三不五時的出現，多聽幾次，自然就會印在腦海裡。

自我訓練建議

一、上 CNN 或 BBC 新聞網下載

在家裡訓練聽力的時候，我建議大家可以上 CNN 或 BBC 新聞網下載新聞 MP3 音檔和腳本檔自我練習。聽下載下來的英文新聞練習時，要養成習慣，注意聽主詞、動詞與斷句處，熟悉它的分段慣性。多聽幾次後，可以嘗試聽寫下來，寫多少算多少，一次次循環將空格處填上直至完整為止。最重要的是，不要忘了跟著複誦的動作。

二、觀看訪談性及脫口秀節目 DVD

另外，我建議大家可以去買或租訪談性以及脫口秀節目的 DVD 來觀看練習。這類節目的對話性很強，是即時性的，不同於念稿的新聞報導，有助於情境式的聽力學習。訪談性節目尤其具有實務性，對於需要與外國人談判時的技巧演練很有幫助。

第一次觀看 DVD 時，建議大家關掉字幕，看完一段，自己寫下大概的內容；第二次聽時，則採一句句播放的方式，仔細聽細節。不要急著一次就整段聽完，可以採每五分鐘的間隔去分段練習，如果非得播放字幕，也一定要選英文字幕，遇到不懂的字就抄下來查字意，跟著複誦記憶。做完這些步驟後，關掉字幕再從頭到尾重聽一次。再提醒一次，一定要留意數字和動詞這些關鍵字。

三、多涉獵大眾文化相關內容

與聽力有關，比較難在短時間內克服的是文化與社會相關資訊，聽力會牽涉到相當多的大眾文化，以及與文化性相關的內容。建議大家平常有空要或多或少自行涉獵，會有助於聽力上的理解。

最後，再為大家針對聽力這個部份的學習做一個整理總結。

1. 將以前學過或以後會遇到的單字全部在腦中轉換成語音，養成錄下來聽與複誦的學習方式。
2. 熟悉語調節奏與斷句處的掌握。
3. 多讀報紙或聽新聞，留意動詞的簡化和名詞的慣用部分。從美式脫口秀中學習隨機性的對話聽力與文化上的指涉。
4. 留意常用的日常俚俗語與慣用語，並熟悉它們。

技巧篇

Listening

Listening

技巧篇前言

　　很多人聽不懂英文的原因包括單字量不足，或是聽到字的聲音而思緒卡住，即使聽了覺得似曾相識但仍然無法連接到字的含意。還有斷句的問題，句中的連音跟語調都會影響聽的專注力，不知哪時該停下來，進而導致聽者不容易抓到重點。本書的技巧篇就是要針對這三個部分來加強練習。

　　關於記憶單字的部分，不是本書的重點，但是必須強調單字的背誦，千萬不能只注意字的拼法而忽略了發音，尤其針對台灣人都只習慣用「看」單字記憶，但這是不夠的，其實「聽」才是正確的方法。背誦單字必須要熟悉發音，而且要唸出來才行。建議將單字或句子自己唸出來或請人唸出並錄音下來，不停地重複聽與唸的動作，重點是要能將字的聲音和它的意義直覺地連結。

　　句子斷句與音調的部分，因為句子不可能一口氣講完，聽的時候要知道哪時要停要斷，在技巧篇中的 Lesson 1、2、6 都有提到相關技巧。要如何快速的掌握英文語句的重要資訊是聽者最終的目的。通常在句子中，重點都在內容字詞上，內容字一般是以名詞動詞居多，有時候具有含意的形容詞副詞也有可能，在 Lesson 4 會做詳細說明。另外否定含意的字眼在聆聽時也容易誤會，需多注意。

　　最後，應付考試必須注意總體應用的技巧，在 Lesson 7~8 有相關說明。考試通常是利用疑問詞的問句來測驗聽者捉住資訊重點的能力，針對技巧篇提出的大方向來練習便能逐漸掌握要領。總結上來說，技巧篇著重的是聲音與節奏的基本規則，必須靠聽者反覆的練習聆聽與口說，光是聽懂是不夠的，一定要自己跟著說，多複誦才能培養對單字的使用與記憶，並獲得紮實的英文聆聽能力。

Lesson 1

停頓

🔑 Part 1. ▶ 要訣：何時停頓

　　一個人在講話時，不論是用何種語言，因為需要呼吸的緣故，不可能不停頓。而在說英文時，停頓出現的情形可分為以下幾種：

一、在提供或強調某個重要關鍵字或訊息之前。
二、根據英文語法結構，在組成的不同部分之間。
三、片語之前。
四、主要子句和附屬子句之間。
五、連接詞之間。
六、在眾多選項之間。

Point 1 在提供或強調某個重要關鍵字或訊息之前

◎ MP3 001

1 She bought some snacks and drinks around seven in the evening with a red-haired boy called ... Ray. （98 年第二次基測）
（她在晚上七點左右買了些零食飲料，跟一個叫 Ray 的紅髮男孩一起。）

....

這句話的重點在於女孩是跟哪一個男孩去約會，所以除了刻意將那個紅髮男孩的姓名放在最後外，在提及之前，會刻意停頓以提高聽者的注意力。

2 The top innovation, the Web, was created by British computer scientist Tim Berners-Lee.

（重大的發明，也就是網路，是由英國電腦科學家 Tim Berners-Lee 創造的。）

☑ innovation（*n.*）改革、創新 ☑ consultant（*n.*）顧問

這句話停頓兩次，停頓後所接的是句子中所要提供的兩個重點訊息，一是重大的發明：the Web，再者是發明者的姓名 Tim Berners-Lee.

3 The magazine in your hand has won 104 Pulitzer Prizes, <u>the most</u> of any news organization.

（你手中的雜誌贏得過 104 座普立茲獎，是所有新聞業中最多的。）

☑ Pulitzer Prize（*n.*）普立茲獎（美國新聞界年度大獎）

☑ organization（*n.*）組織、機構

句中要強調紐約時代雜誌贏得普立茲獎的數目是同業中最多的，提供數字只是證明資料的可信度，所以講到「最多」時，要先停頓以表明強調的重點。

Point 2 根據英文語法結構，依組成的不同部分加以切割停頓

◎ MP3 002

1 One day, the people in her town get sick in a strange way.

（98 年第一次基測）

（有一天，她城鎮裡的人生了很奇怪的病。）

一個句子，不論長短，都會按語法結構的分段來做輕微的停頓。以這句為例，我們可以將之切割為四部分，斜線的地方就是稍做停頓處：

One day, / the people in her town / get sick / in a strange way.

　時間　/　　　主詞　　　/　動詞　/　　片語

一般而言，一個最基本的英文句子是由主詞、動詞、受詞所構成，也有可能多一點資訊包括時間和地點。而這些基本構成單位不一定是一個單字，也常可能是由片語構成。在分析拆解句子的結構時，必須對英文句子結構有基礎的了解。

2 I heard / there are many monkeys / on this mountain.

（98 年第一次基測）

（我聽說這座山上有許多猴子。）

....

I 是主詞而 heard 是動詞，因為這兩部分都是一個字，所以中間就可省略了停頓。there are many monkeys 是一子句當受詞用，所以同為一個部分。最後一部分就是代表地點的片語。

3 A good speaker / should display / his learning / to the audience / in an enthusiastic way.（94 年指考）

（一個好的演講者 / 應該呈現 / 他的所學 / 給聽眾 / 以鼓舞人心的方式。）

☑ audience（*n.*）觀眾

....

按結構將句子分為五個部分分隔，分別為：主詞 / 動詞 / 受詞 / 介系詞片語 / 介系詞片語，中間分隔處就會有輕微的停頓。

Point 3 片語之前

◎ MP3 **003**

1 She is very good at singing / and has won many prizes / in the past few years / with her beautiful voice.（98 年第二次基測）

（她非常善於唱歌並在過去幾年用她的美麗歌聲贏過許多獎項。）

....

片語在句子的結構中屬於一個單獨的部分，按照句型結構，本就可能稍做停頓。有時每個單位因為字數太少會連音的關係，並不是每次都會停頓，但是遇到片語，絕大多數都是會停頓的。以此句為例，主詞 She 和第一個動詞所帶的子句裡每個字都很短，所以可以連著一起念，遇到連接詞 and 便停頓，接下來的兩個片語 in the past few years 和 with her beautiful voice 之前都有明顯的停頓。

2 Today, / with a couple of clicks, / you can go anywhere in the world / without leaving your computer. （94 年指考）

（今日，按幾次滑鼠，你就可以去世界的任何地方而不離開你的電腦。）

⊘click（*n.*）卡嚓聲（一般指按滑鼠的聲音）

....

劃線的部分為片語。第一個字 today 放在開頭想要強調現今的時代，之後因為接著是一個副詞片語，故馬上停頓一下，中間的主要句子因主詞、動詞、受詞簡短所以可以連成一氣，但接著又是一個副詞片語，所以又停了一下。

3 The annual meeting / of the Board of Trustees / of Mountains College / will be held / at 10 a.m. / on May 20th / in the Main Conference Room.

（群山大學信託管理部門年會將於五月二十日早上十點在主會議室舉行。）

⊘annual（*adj.*）年度的　⊘Board of Trustees（*n.*）信託管理部門
⊘conference（*n.*）會議

....

這句話中含有許多片語構成的資訊，主詞 the annual meeting 之後接的地點、時間、所屬單位等等都是片語，所以在講的時候必須停頓以清楚的表達資訊。

MP3 004

1 Molly Wilson is a shy little girl / who lives in Glass Town.
（98 年第二次基測）

（Molly Wilson 是個住在 Glass Town 的害羞女生。）

一個句子裡的停頓主要是以組成句子的結構來分段，而如果一個句子裡含有不只一個子句，當然在兩個子句之間，會停頓以示區別。以這句為例，從 who 開始便是形容詞子句，以 who 來引導，所以在 who 之前，語氣就會先停頓表示接下來的是一個子句。

2 Most of the accidents happened / because drivers didn't follow the traffic rules.（90 年第一次基測）

（大部分意外的發生是因為駕駛人沒有遵守交通規則。）

不只是修飾名詞的形容詞子句，其他表條件、因果關係的子句等，在另一個子句開始前，語氣都會停頓。這句話中 because 後接著的是表示原因的子句，所以會在 because 前停頓。

3 Though Dr. Wang has been away from his hometown for over ten years, / he can still visualize his old house clearly.（94 年指考）

（雖然王醫師已經離開他的家鄉超過十年，他仍然能清楚描繪出他老家的景象。）

☑ visualize（v.）視覺化

這句話是由因果關係構成的兩個子句，很明顯地停頓處是落在兩個子句之間。

Point 5 連接詞之間

◎ MP3 005

1 It is fun / and exciting to visit different countries / and meet different people.（90 年第一次基測）

（拜訪不同的國家以及和不同的人見面是既有趣又刺激的。）

連接詞中最常用的就是 and、but 和 or，遇到連接詞時，語氣都會停頓一下再接著說出另一個對等的選項。本句中出現兩次 and，第一次連接兩個形容詞，第二次連接兩個動作。停頓的時間點也就是在這兩個 and 之前。

2 I don't know for sure / what I am going to do / this weekend, / but tentatively I plan to visit an old friend of mine / in southern Taiwan.（94 年指考）

（我不確定我這周末要做什麼，但目前可能是計畫去拜訪我在南台灣的一位老友。）

☑ tentatively（*adv.*）暫時地

這句話中的連接詞 but 連接兩個句子，但不論子句中是否停頓，遇到連接詞之前都會停一下，再接下一個子句。

Point 6 在眾多選項之間

◎ MP3 006

1 I have made several new friends. They are from different countries: Japan, / Germany, /. and Russia.（90 年第一次基測）

（我交了些新朋友。他們來自不同的國家，有日本、德國和俄國。）

當句子中出現超過兩個選項時，每個選項之間都會有短暫停頓。（只有兩個選項時會有連接詞，因此也會停頓。）

2 One can generally judge the quality of eggs with the naked eye. Externally, good eggs must be clean, / free of cracks, / and smooth-shelled. （98 年指考）

（一個人可以大略的用肉眼評判蛋的品質。從外表看，好的蛋肯定是乾淨、沒有裂痕且外殼平滑的。）

☑generally（*adv.*）一般地　☑naked（*adj.*）赤裸的

☑externally（*adv.*）外在地　☑crack（*n.*）裂痕

☑smooth-shelled（*adj.*）外殼光滑的

選項不論多少個，每個之間都會停頓，此外，選項也不一定都是名詞，也可能是形容詞、動詞或句子，但都是對等的。不論選項的長短，還是會加以分隔停頓。這句話中的三個選項，都是形容詞，雖然字數並不一致，但仍不影響停頓的時機。

3 We then put on a pot of coffee, / eat some more farina, / and sit chatting about our dreams / after the expedition / when life starts again.

（我們於是拿出一壺咖啡，吃一些穀粉，並坐著聊我們完成這趟遠征後的夢想，那時可是人生的另一個開始。）

☑farina（*n.*）穀粉　☑expedition（*n.*）遠征、探險

這句話中的多選項是數個動作，並在一開始就呈現。接連三個選項後，再跟著片語及子句切割分段。雖然每個選項都是動詞與受詞，但因為字數少所以用正常口語速度敘述時，並不會停頓。

上述英文句子出現停頓的情形，彼此間並不互相牴觸，而是都以句法結構為原則分割停頓，再加上其他情形互相調整而分段。所以熟悉分解句子結構並多做口語練習，句子停頓的時機與節奏並不難掌握。

Part2。綜合範例

◎ MP3 007

1 **The woman / and man / will go to dinner / and a classical music concert / on Saturday evening.**

（這對男女在星期六晚上將去吃晚餐，而後去古典音樂會。）

假設由一個說話很慢的人來唸，根據句子結構分段以及遇到連接詞都會停頓。兩個連接詞 and 之前都會停一下，主詞 The woman and man 後停一下，動詞跟緊連著的受詞 will go to dinner 之後停，另外在句尾的時間片語 on Saturday evening 前也會停頓。

2 **Before going shopping, / Dad asked me / if Mom would eat at home tonight. / He wanted to know / what he should buy / for dinner.** （100 年第二次基測）

（在去購物前，爸爸問我，媽媽今晚是否在家吃晚餐。他想要知道他要買什麼當晚餐。）

本段結構為：時間片語 / 主詞動詞受詞 / if 子句 . / 主詞動詞 / what 子句 / 片語。嚴格說來，根據結構，Dad asked me 跟第二句的 He wanted to know 都可以再切割，但因為字不多所以可以連著唸不需停頓。這兩句話可以分成六小段，但也因人而異，有人念很快也是可以停的更少。

3 **I'm sorry to learn that / some of them / don't really enjoy biking / or get hurt / on the road / because they don't prepare well.** （99 年第一次基測）

（知道他們之中的一些人因為沒有準備妥當而沒有真正享受騎單車或是在路上受傷，我感到很遺憾。）

....

這句話中的停頓點首先是在 that 後接一個子句時。再者，子句中的主詞比較長，有三個字 some of them，所以停一下再接動詞 don't really enjoy biking。連接詞 or 連接兩個動作，在連接詞之前，我們一定也會再停頓。接著是片語 on the road 前的停頓。because 後接原因的子句，所以在它之前，也會停頓。

4 **If you exercise regularly, / your blood circulation will improve / and you will feel more energetic.** （94 年指考）

（如果你規律運動，你的血液循環就會改進，而你也會覺得更有活力。）

☑ regularly（*adv.*）規律地　☑ circulation（*n.*）循環
☑ improve（*v.*）進步、改善　☑ energetic（*adj.*）精力旺盛的

....

不同的子句之間當然是會停頓，不管是因果、假設或關係子句都是相同的道理。這句話中首先在表示條件的子句和主要子句間停頓，之後主要子句裡又有連接詞接另一個句子，所以在連接詞 and 前也會停頓。又因為這個句子中的主詞動詞的字都不多，所以可以連在一起念，不用按每個結構都分段停頓。

5 **We will do / all we can / to find / and punish them / in accordance with our laws, / and we will destroy them / if they offer resistance.** (改寫自 CNN.com)

（我們將會盡我們所能找出他們並依我們的法律懲罰之，如果他們做出反抗我們也會毀掉他們。）

✅ punish（*v.*）處罰　✅ in accordance with（*ph.*）與⋯⋯一致

✅ destroy（*v.*）摧毀、破壞　✅ resistance（*n.*）抵抗

⋯⋯⋯⋯⋯⋯⋯⋯⋯⋯⋯⋯⋯⋯⋯⋯⋯⋯⋯⋯⋯⋯⋯⋯⋯⋯⋯⋯⋯⋯⋯⋯⋯⋯⋯⋯⋯⋯⋯

這句話雖然有一點長，但經過結構拆解以及之前提過的停頓要點來分析，句意和重點其實不難了解。以下分段解釋：**We will do**〔主詞＋動詞〕（我們將會做）/ **all we can**〔受詞片語〕（所有我們能夠的）/ **to find / and punish them**〔因為有 and 連接詞所以停一下〕（去找出並懲罰他們）/ **in accordance with our laws**〔片語〕（根據我們的法律）/ **and we will destroy them**〔又是因為連接詞 and 所以停住，再接子句〕（並且我們將摧毀他們）/ **if they offer resistance**〔條件子句〕（如果他們做出反抗）。

Part 3. 練習題 【詳解請見 p202】

請聆聽以下的句子，找出句中的停頓點並劃斜線表示。

◎ MP3 008

❶ Just go down Market Road for two blocks and turn left.（98 年第二次基測）

❷ Sometimes she sits by the window looking at the flowers in the garden.（98 年第二次基測）

❸ The doctor says that it is impossible for her to go to school today.（90 年第一次基測）

❹ There's a pretty good barber shop near my house.

❺ The kid is holding his bicycle seat and handle bars.

❻ The most convenient way to get around this small town is to ride a bike.（100 年第一次基測）

❼ The patient responds verbally or with gestures to indicate emotions such as pain, stress or anxiety.（98 年指考）

❽ He and five other boys took turns jumping rope for two and half hours and collected more than US$1,200 in donations for the American Heart Association.（98 年指考）

❾ In ancient Egypt, as long ago as 1500 BC, outward appearance expressed a person's status, role in society, and political position.（98 年指考）

⑩ We have had plenty of rain so far this year, so there should be an abundant supply of fresh water this summer.（94 年指考）

⑪ The crimes, like the one that was committed in northern Cambodia today, are aimed at sowing enmity between our citizens.

⑫ Beginning with Toy Story in 1995, pixar has produced eleven feature films, all of which have met with critical and commercial success. （改寫自 www.dailyblam.com）

⑬ Flags on all regional buildings will fly at half-staff and all entertainment programs on local TV will be cancelled as well as concerts and theater performances.（摘錄自 childrenstargroups.blogspot.com）

⑭ As of 2010, this film, it could be said, was the most successful film in history.

⑮ A girl with her own views will perhaps be able to more quickly and effectively solve life's problems.

Lesson 2
重音與語調

🔑 Part 1. ▸ 要訣：高低起伏的音調變化

　　英文和中文在口語上最大的不同就是，英文不論字或句都有高低起伏音調的變化。因為不熟悉這些起起伏伏的口氣與節奏，才會導致聽不清楚英文的內容。而造成語音起伏的原因主要有兩部分：

一、重音：A. 通常在字的第一音節
　　　　　B. 內容字重於功能字
二、語調：A. 直述句＝肯定的，敘述事實或事件。
　　　　　B. 疑問句＝詢問別人或表示疑問。
　　　　　C. 否定句＝加入 not 或 hardly 等字，表示否定含義。

　　首先，重音與語調的差別，根據劍橋英文字典的解釋，重音 (stress) 的含意是指一個字或音節發音比其他字或音節來的重且強。

" when a word or syllable is pronounced with greater force than other words in the same sentence or other syllables in the same word."

　　而語調 (intonation) 則是指在說話時聲音音調或高或低的轉變；尤其在話語的含意上有所影響，例如非疑問句的句子最終通常會有明顯的往下音調。

" the sound changes produced by the rise and fall of the voice when speaking, especially when this has an effect on the meaning of what is said. The end of a sentence that is not a question is usually marked by falling intonation."

（摘錄自 *Cambridge Advanced Learner's Dictionary*）

從這兩類引起語音高低起伏的原因來分析，英文每個字裡，都會有輕音節跟重音節的差別，所以念起來會有抑揚頓挫。而英文句子裡，除了遇到上一章節所提到的停頓（停頓前語氣會稍微往上升，停頓完後會往下降），以及疑問句或驚嘆句之外，**一般情形，英文的語氣都是往下走的**。以下便分為重音跟語調兩部分進行更仔細的解說。

＊符號說明：① 有　　　　色底效果的地方，表示須作重音。② 灰色線條 ⌒ ↘ 代表語調上揚或下沈。

Point 1　重音

◎ MP3 009

A. 通常在字的第一音節

　　一般來說，英文字的結構大都是前音節而非次音節，也就是說，大部分的英文字都是以第一個音節為重音節，如 exercise、regularly、mental、physical，但也有少數的字重音在後面第二音節，如 performance 和 alarming。

　　而需要特別注意的是有些字會因為詞類不同而重音節位置不同。例如 increase, suspect, contract, permit, digest, survey 等等；這些字當名詞時重音在前，當動詞時重音在後。例如：

1 Regular exercise helps to **increase** your mental and physical performance.
（規律運動有助於增加你心智與身體的效能。）

2 The sharp **increase** in his weight during the last three months is alarming.

（他這三個月體重的劇烈增加是令人擔憂的。）

以上兩句話中的 increase，第一個是動詞（重音在後），而第二句的則是名詞（重音在前）。

B. 內容字重於功能字

除了單字本身有輕重音節，句子裡的每個字也會有相對輕或重的音。例如句子中的關鍵字一定是加重音以提醒注意。句子中的內容字，一般包括名詞、動詞、形容詞、副詞，都是會發出較重的音；而介系詞（如 on、in、at）、冠詞（the、a）及代名詞（如 he、she、they）則屬於不加重的輕音字。在說句子時，字跟字之間的輕重對比很明顯地造成了句子的音調不同與高低起伏。例如：

3 Some people are walking along the street.
（有些人正在街上走。）

加上底色的音節是屬於內容字，必須加重音，而其他字相對而言就比較輕且小聲。

4 On cold days, my cats love to lie on the couch because it is warm and comfortable. （96 年第一次基測）
（冷天時，我的貓咪們喜歡躺在沙發椅上因為它溫暖又舒服。）
⊘ couch（*n.*）長沙發、躺椅

標重音的內容字一般就是主導句子主要含意的字；比較輕音的字，很容易因為小聲或連音帶過導致聽不清楚，但只要能捉住屬於較重音的字意，也就已經能了解該句的重點。如這句的 cold、cats、lie、couch、warm 以及 comfortable，聽到這些字，即使沒有聽清楚所有的字，也能自行猜測出上下文大致的含意。

◎ MP3 010

分為三種情形：直述句、疑問句、否定句

A. 直述句

英文句子一般是越後面越重，語調是往下降的。如果句子比較長，分成兩部分，第一個部分語氣會先往上，第二部分再往下，所以當有人講英文句子時語氣往上揚，就代表他話還沒有講完，後面還會接著語氣往下降的句子。

1 Many people say that e-mail is just a faster way to deliver letters. （95 年指考）

（許多人說電子郵件只是一種比較迅速的傳遞郵件方式。）

☑ deliver（v.）遞送

直述句不論長短，不管中間的抑揚頓挫起起伏伏，語氣最終都是往下沉的。

2 Many of my classmates have had the experience of taking an airplane, but I haven't. （96 年第一次基測）

（我有許多同學都有搭飛機的經驗，但我沒有。）

一個句子裡有兩個子句時，通常第一個子句結束前語氣會微微上揚，接下來完結的子句會再落下。這句話因為語意上後面的子句持相反的含意，字也較少，所以語氣更明顯地重重落下。

B. 疑問句

只要是表示疑問的句子，不管是否倒裝，語氣通常是往上揚的。 所以聽到語氣往上揚的句子，不是疑問句就是尚未講完的直述句。

3 Is your sister still living in Berlin?
（你姊姊還是住在柏林嗎？）
....
一般問句結尾會很明顯的語氣上揚，所以一聽就知道句子含有疑問的性質。

4 Isn't the loading dock next to the back entrance?
（貨物下載區不是在後門邊嗎？）
✅ loading dock（n.）裝載貨物的碼頭或平台

問句有很多形式，這句話是否定疑問句，但不論是哪種疑問法語氣都會上揚。

5 You've studied English for a long time, haven't you?
（93 年第二次基測）
（你研讀英文已經有很長一段時間了，對嗎？）
....
附加疑問句的形式也是一樣會語氣上揚。

C. 驚嘆句

這種句子比較短，且重音都在前面。

6 Be careful!（小心！）
....
通常驚嘆句字數都較少，重音放在前面有提醒人注意的作用。

7 Stop at the corner! (在轉角停！)

這句驚嘆句的重音重重地在落第一個字上。比較另外相似的兩句就可以很明顯的聽出語調在不同種類句子的起伏。

Can you stop at the corner? (你可以在轉角停下來嗎？)

You can stop at the corner. (你可以在轉角停下來。)

相似的字但用在不同的語句，語調就不同。第一句問句的語氣往上揚；第二句直述句往下落。

　　總結而言，聽英文的時候，關於語氣，要把握幾個原則：第一：英文字的輕重，一般都在字的單字前面比較重；而句子中具有含意的內容字會重，其他字會輕，由這些輕輕重重的字構成一些高低起伏。第二：由這些起起伏伏構成的句子，又會因為整句語氣的三個情形：① 直述句往下，或先往上再往下；② 疑問句會往上；③ 驚嘆句重音會在前。英文的語調就是結合這些原則而有起伏。

Part 2. 綜合範例

根據本單元的技巧原則，仔細聽發重音的字，以及語調上揚或下沉的地方。若該句沒有明顯的語調起伏，即注意重音即可。

* 符號說明：① 有 ▢ 灰底效果的地方，表示須作重音。② 灰色線條 ⟍ 代表語調上揚或下沉。

◎ MP3 011

1 When you leave the room, please turn off the light.

（當你離開房間時，請關燈。）

標重音的是句子中音比較重的內容字，通常聽到這些重音的字就能拼湊出句意。而這句話雖然是直述句，但 when 開頭的前面子句的語氣有微微上揚，然後接下來的子句語氣最後會往下落。

2 Whichever ship you choose, you will have a wonderful experience seeing the best of Europe this year.

（無論你挑哪一艘船，今年你都將會看到歐洲最棒的一面並擁有一個美好的經驗。）

語氣上一開始會往上揚，最後再往下降，這是一般較長的直述句都有的情形。而字跟字之間的音調起伏就只要記得將內容字用重一點的音，其他字輕輕說出就可以有英文抑揚頓挫的起伏。有灰底的字是加重音的字（若是兩個音節以上，需要加重音的音節才有灰底，大部分都是在第一音節）。

3 **She now** knows **how** **people look is** not **the same as** what **they really are.** (100 年第一次基測)

（她現在知道人們看起來的樣子跟他們真實自我是不一樣的。）

··

一般而言內容字都會稍微加重音，如本句的動詞 knows。名詞也是屬於含有意義的內容字，但在這句話中的受詞不是明顯的名詞而是疑問詞帶領的片語，如 how people look 以及 what they really are，所以這兩個疑問詞都會加重音以強調其作為受詞的含意。而 not the same 也需稍微加重音表示「不同」的意思。同時，此句為肯定句所以句尾語氣下沉。

4 **I** don't **know much about** science **, but I** do **know I would** hate **to live on a planet full of** copies of me. (100 年第二次基測)

（我不太懂科學，但我確知我會厭惡生活在一個充滿和我一樣的複製品的星球。）

··

重音的規則普遍而言只要把握住將有含意的內容字（即動詞、名詞）稍重音，再根據語意做一些調整即可。例如這句的動詞名詞為：don't know、do know、science、hate to live、planet 以及 copies，都加重音。因為 do know 和 don't know 具有相反意思所以要加重音以強調不同；hate to live 兩個動詞因為 hate 較有情緒的感覺且在前面，所以 hate 的重音要比較重些，其他內容字就稍微加重就可以了。這句雖屬直述句，但分成兩段，所以在 but 之前沒有明顯下降的語氣，而在末端 copies of me 時才有明顯下降語氣。

技巧篇

5 Noah: I've had **too** many cookies. My throat is **so dry**.

Quinn: **What** would you like to **drink** then?

Noah: **Any thing** you can **get**. Just **get** it **Now**!

（100 年第二次基測）

（Noah: 我吃了太多餅乾，我喉嚨好乾。

Quinn: 那麼你想要喝點什麼？

Noah: 任何你可以拿的都好，只要現在快點拿來！）

這幾句對話中重音不難找，只要含有意義的都稍微加重，但因為字不多，明顯加重的只有需要特別強調的 too many、so dry、anything、now。注意語氣方面的差別，這些句子語氣都屬下沉，頭兩句因為也加重音，所以下沉最明顯。最後一句的命令句雖然尾字 now 要強調，但有點驚嘆的口氣，所以開頭會加重。另外，這裡的疑問句沒有語氣上揚，詳細原因請看 Lesson 7。

Part 3. 練習題 【詳解請見 p203】

請聆聽以下的句子，找出發重音的字，並畫出語調上揚或下沈的記號。

◎ MP3 **012**

❶ As opportunities in Asia grow, so will East Line's ways of getting you there.

❷ Have you ever cooked chicken on the grill?

❸ You are going on vacation, aren't you?

❹ In your opinion, what kind of printer should we buy?

❺ When will the boss be able to arrange to meet us, then?

❻ How can I get to the hotel from the airport?

❼ Couldn't you possibly give us a more specific suggestion?

❽ His company is located on the 27th floor, office 27G.

❾ Should I get the blue one?

❿ While he was swimming in the sea, his mother just stood by watching him.

⓫ Pack now and get ready to be COOL!（100 年第二次基測）

⓬ Worried about catching a cold? You don't have to be.（100 年第二次基測）

⑬ Kelly: Have you read the news about the Cine Prize nominations?

Eunice: Yeah. I can't believe *Took Off* got the most nominations. It's not that good.（100 年第一次基測）

⑭ Last month, a hacker who identified himself as "Gabriel" claimed to have broken into the computer system of the British publisher of *Harry Potter*.（摘錄自 www.breitbart.com）

⑮ As thousands of new immigrants from Southeastern Asia have moved to Taiwan for work or marriage, we should try our best to help them adjust to our society.

Lesson 3

口語的省略

🔑 Part 1. 要訣：常省略的字

英文不像中文每一個字都會清清楚楚念出來，它是種有節奏的語言，可分為有聲字跟無聲字。區分的第一個原則是造成語氣抑揚頓挫的輕重音，第二個則是根據發音的規則，會有省略不唸或連音的字。以下將容易省略的情形列為五種：

一、Be 動詞及助動詞
二、代名詞
三、介系詞
四、連接詞
五、其他變化（如 -ing）

Point 1 　Be 動詞及助動詞

🎧 MP3 013

口語上，Be 動詞和助動詞都會省略部分而和前面的字連音；這裡指的 Be 動詞和助動詞有 am、are、is、was、were、will、do、does、did、would、have、has 和 had 等等，在句子中這些字都會省略而與前面或後面的字連音。例如：

1 I am fine. → *I'm*
（我很好。）

2 I have been to Egypt before. → *I've*
（我之前去過埃及。）

3 We would like to talk to you. → *we'd*

（我們想要跟你說話。）

··

有時 Be 動詞和助動詞在省略時，不一定都和前面的字連音，也可能與後面的字連音，例如在句首表示疑問或是否定時和後面的 not 連音。

4 Does she live in Taipei? → *duh-she*

（她住在台北嗎？）

5 Did they live near you? → *dih-they*

（他們住在你附近嗎？）

6 Why will you need a large hat? → *why'll*

（你為何需要一頂大帽子？）

7 He has not arrived yet. → *he's not* 或 *he hasn't*

（他還沒有抵達。）

··

否定句的時候，Be 動詞和助動詞在省略時有兩種選擇，可以和前面主詞或後面 not 連音。

8 I should have gone there by train. → *shoulda*

（我應該要搭火車去的。）

··

Should, could, would, must, may, might 後面加上 have 時因為省略 have，發音時會有變化，會變成字尾加 a 音，如果是加 have not 則會變成字尾加 na 音。

◎ MP3 014

　　這裡所指的代名詞不只包括 I、you、he、she、we、they、it，還有所有格代名詞 my、yours、his、her、our、their、its，以及受格代名詞 me、you、him、her、us、them。在這些代名詞中，you、your、yours 最容易省略，而 he、his、her、him 這些 h 開頭的音也很容易在句子裡省略 h 不發音。

1 What are you talking about? → *ya*

（你在說什麼？）

除非是要強調 you，否則 you 在句中都是用輕音 ya 省略帶過。

2 Wow! You're so tall now. → *yer*

（哇！你現在這麼高啊！）

your 或 you're 在省略時會變為輕音的 yer。

3 I've sent his package. → *is*

（我寄了他的包裹。）

4 I saw them yesterday. → *saw 'em*

（我昨天看到他們。）

5 Don't you think she is pretty? → *don't cha*

（你不覺得她很漂亮嗎？）

you 和 your 如果遇到前面字的字尾是 t 或 d 時，因為省略又連音造成的發音上的變化。遇到 t 會變音為 cha 和 cher，遇到 d 會變為 ja 和 jer。

Point 3 介系詞

　　一般來說，介系詞在句子裡都會輕音帶過，其中最明顯的就是 to、for 和 of：to 都會念成 tu 或 da 連著前面或後面的字發音。for 省略時會念成 fer 或 fe。of 則會念成 u 或 a，f 的音就會省略不唸。

1 They used to live in Taipei. → *used-u*
（他們以前住在台北。）

....

因為 d 和 t 兩音連音。

2 I left one for you. → *fe*
（我留一個給你。）

3 She is a friend of mine. → *a-mine*
（她是我的一個朋友。）

Point 4 連接詞

⊚ MP3 **016**

　　連接詞中最容易也最明顯的省略字就是 and 與 or，一方面連接詞本身就容易讓人忽略，再者是因為這兩個字都是母音開頭，所以特別容易省略及連音到其他字上。另外如 because 也會在念很快時省略為 'cause。

1 I need a pen and a pencil. → *a pen-n-a pencil*
（我需要一隻鉛筆跟筆。）

....

and 會省略只唸 n 的音並連接前面和後面兩個相等地位的詞。

2 Which one do you want? Coffee or tea? → coffee-*er* tea
（你要哪一個？咖啡還是茶？）

相對於 and，or 會唸成輕音 er 並只連接前面的詞。

3 John and I saw a movie in the theater last night because we got free tickets. → John-*n*-I, *'cause*
（約翰跟我昨晚在電影院看了一場電影，因為我們有免費票。）

Point 5 其他變化

◎ MP3 017

　　其他容易省略的字有字尾是 ing 時，在唸的時候會省略為 'in，而只要是 h 開頭的字，口語上都會將 h 的音省略。另外還有 can 和 can't 在句子裡和其他字連音時會變音成為 kin 和 kant。還有一些由上面情形綜合而成的變化，由以下例子來看一些其他情形：

1 What're you doing? → *do-in'*
（你在做什麼？）

2 Are you happy with the end? → *'appy*
（你對結局感到高興嗎？）

3 I can sing, but I can't write songs. → *kin, kant*
（我會唱歌但是我不會寫歌。）

4 What do you need? → *whaddaya*
（你需要什麼？）

do 和 you 都是會省略的字，遇在一起的時候會全都連在一起，唸 whaddaya。

5 I'm <u>going to</u> pay the bill. → *gonna*
（我要去付帳。）

to 很容易省略而與其他字連音，為了方便唸下一個音，t 會用 n 的音帶過，而 o 的音會唸作 a，所以 going to 會變成 gonna，want to 會變成 wanna。

6 I <u>want to</u> see the menu. → *wanna*
（我要看菜單。）

⚪ Part2. 綜合範例

邊聽邊念，感覺並練習口語的省略！雖然可能不習慣，但實際口語唸起來確實就是如此。

在做練習時，請一句一句聽，跟讀複誦，切記一定要多唸出聲來，多聽多唸才會習慣，也才能聽懂。

◎ MP3 **018**

1 **What are you thinking of having for lunch?**
→ [Whaddaya ∶ thinkin' a ∶ havin' fer]

（你有想到要吃什麼午餐嗎？）

2 **I had to stay at home or in the hospital.**
→ [I 'ad ta ∶ home-er]

（我必須待在家或醫院。）

3 A: Is that your brother? The tall man in front of the jackets?
B: Yes, he is looking for a jacket for work.
→ [yer ∶ a] [he's ∶ lookin' fer ∶ fer]

（A: 那是你哥哥嗎？那個站在夾克前面的男人？ B: 是的。他正在找一件工作用的夾克。）

4 Kathleen: I really have to go.
Joe: Yeah, well, you don't want to be late. （電影 *You've Got Mail* 電子情書）
→ [have-tu] [wanna]

（Kathleen: 我真的必須走了。Joe: 嗯，是啊，你不會想要遲到的。）

5 Jane: Ned hasn't <u>talked to</u> me <u>for</u> two days <u>because</u> I <u>laughed at his</u> hair color. What should I do?

Lois: You should <u>go and tell him</u> that <u>you're</u> sorry. He's nice, <u>and I'm</u> sure he'll give <u>you another</u> chance.

（100 年第一次基測）

→ [talk-tu；fe；'cause；laugh-ta 's]
  [go-n-tell'm；yer；n-I'm；y-another]

（Jane: Ned 已經兩天因為我取笑他的髮色而沒有跟我說話了。我該怎麼辦？
Lois: 你應該去跟他道歉。他人很好，我很確定他會再給你機會的。）

Part 3. 練習題 【詳解請見 p205】

把可能省略的字都先找出來後，再試著連音。

◎ MP3 **019**

❶ Do you like the Internet?

❷ She had finished her homework at 8:00.

❸ There is a room for children and babies.

❹ Do you want a yellow coat or a red one?

❺ Why has she gone to New York?

❻ I must have been crazy to try to find his house out here.

❼ What do you want to do that for?

❽ Why are you doing this now? You should have done it a few days ago.

❾ A: Hello! What have you been doing lately?
B: Oh, I've been hiking a lot. So, where has your sister been? I haven't seen her.

❿ A: What do we need to buy?
B: Well, a couple of bottles of water, some sandwiches, and chocolate… Wait! I don't have my credit card. Do you have yours?

⓫ Life is like a box of chocolates. You never know what you're going to get. (電影 *Forrest Gump* 阿甘正傳)

⑫ She's worried about this document getting there late.

⑬ You're really crazy to go swimming in the lake on a cold winter day. Don't you feel cold?（100 年第一次基測）

⑭ What am I going to do? I don't even know what is happening right now.

⑮ I've loved you more than I've ever loved any woman and I've waited for you longer than I've ever waited for any woman.（電影 *Gone with the Wind* 亂世佳人）

Lesson 4

內容字詞與功能字詞

 **Part 1。**
要訣：區分「內容字詞」與「功能字詞」

　　英文句子中的字可以根據含意分為內容字詞和功能字詞兩類，之前在分別輕重音的技巧單元已初步介紹過。但是那是針對發音的部分解釋，本單元所要針對的是英文字對句子語意中的關係。內容字詞是建構出語意的重要部分，而功能字詞雖然也會影響到句意，但不是絕對的因素。區分內容字詞與功能字詞，根據詞性，可以分為三類：

一、內容字詞：名詞、動詞
二、功能字詞：介系詞、助動詞、Be 動詞、連接詞、冠詞及單複數、
　　　代名詞
三、介於兩者之間：形容詞、副詞

Point 1　內容字詞

◎ MP3 020

　　英文的內容字詞包含句子含意的主要來源，一般都落在名詞跟動詞上。尤其是口語溝通，大部分時候，只要能聽懂句中的名詞和動詞的含意，句子整體的意義便能顯現。 雖然稱為動詞，但助動詞與 Be 動詞並不屬於內容字而是屬於功能性字詞，其本身並不實質影響意義。

1 Check the traffic and weather news.（99 年第一次基測）
（查詢交通及氣象新聞。）

光是看動詞和名詞就能知道這句話的主要含意。動詞 check（檢視查詢）和名詞 traffic（交通）、weather news（氣象新聞），這些內容字就是語意的來源。

2 **We'll have Tony and Sophie to help us soon.**（99 年第一次基測）

（我們將很快地得到 Tony 和 Sophie 的幫助。）

....

暫且不論其他字詞，只注意此句的名詞和動詞，Tony 和 Sophie 以及 have 和 help，就可以連想到這兩人與「擁有」、「幫助」等含意。

Point 2 功能字詞

◎ MP3 **021**

除了名詞和動詞以外，其他的詞性相對而言對於句子語意的貢獻就不那麼重要。這類型的字詞在句子裡主要用以連結並架構句子裡的各個元素，對於理解句子雖然有其重要性，但本身影響句意的程度不多，所以稱為功能性字詞。它們包括：

▷ 介系詞：**of**、**at**、**with**、**in**、**on**、**for** 等等
▷ 助動詞：**do**、**did**、**can**、**would**、**should** 等等
▷ Be 動詞：**is**、**are**、**was**、**were**、**been** 等等
▷ 連接詞：**and**、**or**、**but**、**because** 等等
▷ 冠詞：**a**、**an**、**the** 等等
▷ 表示單複數的詞：**a lot of**、**many** 等等
▷ 代名詞：**he**、**she**、**they**、**his**、**her**、**its**、**us**、**them** 等等

稍微不同的是，在這些字詞中，代名詞（包括 he、she、we、they 等

人稱代名詞、my、your、his、her 等所有格代名詞或 him、her、them 等
受格）雖然是功能字，因為帶有句中名詞的含意，所以仍會稍微影響語意。

1 When I was walking along the river, I saw some fish jumping
out of the water.（96 年第二次基測）

（當我正沿著河走著，我看見一些魚從水中跳出來。）

劃線的字是功能字詞，他們的含意只有顯示句子的時間 when、was，以
及地點的一些相對位置如 along、out of，或是表示約略數量的 some，
我們無法從這些字得知句子想表達的意思，同時他們也不會影響到句子
的語意。

2 We'll have Tony and Sophie to help us soon.（99 年第一次基測）

（我們將很快地得到 Tony 和 Sophie 的幫助。）

這是前面內容字詞的第二個例句，同一句話我們已經知道其內容字是在
動詞跟名詞，其他的字在此屬於功能性，例如助動詞 will 連接詞 and 等
等，本身的含意並不會影響到句意，只是顯示時間是未來，以及連接兩
個名詞的 and，是標準的功能性字詞。但這裡的代名詞 we 跟 us，代表
的是主詞我們 we 以及受幫助的受詞 us，不能說完全不影響句子，仍是
會有些許影響。

Point 3 介於兩者之間

◎ MP3 022

形容詞跟副詞並不屬於前兩者的範圍，它們一般而言是具有內容性的，
但其功能性與內容性的多寡沒有一定準則，必須靠句子中的其他字來做判
斷。有時同一個形容詞或副詞在不同的句子裡可能會有不同的性質，完全

要看它是否會影響到句子語意。

1 Do you have any available for <u>immediate</u> delivery?
（你有現貨可以馬上送嗎？）

☑ available（*adj.*）有空的　☑ immediate（*adj.*）立即的

形容詞 immediate 雖然有描寫急迫的意思，但根據內容字詞顯示這句話要表示詢問是否有貨可以送，所以這個形容詞在這句話中是功能性大於內容性的。

2 Making a U-turn on this street is <u>illegal</u>.
（在這條路迴轉是違規的。）

☑ illegal（*adj.*）非法的

這句話的形容詞 illegal（不合法的），顯示句中動作的性質。因為這句話中的內容字動詞是 Be 動詞，並非有語意的一般動詞，所以內容落在形容詞上，故以這句的例子，這個形容詞的內容性大於功能性。

3 Check every part of your bike <u>carefully</u>.（99 年第一次基測）
（仔細檢查你腳踏車的每一個部分。）

副詞 carefully（仔細地）是要形容動作 check（檢查）的狀態，含有的意義不能完全被忽略，所以這句的副詞具有內容性，但是它的內容性仍不比動作 check 重要。

4 Mom, come home quick. The dog's <u>really</u> sick!
（媽媽快回來，小狗生病了。）

這句話裡有兩個副詞 quick（快）和 really（真地），第一個子句裡的內

68

容字動詞 come 表示「來」，但無法表現出急迫的感覺，所以副詞 quick 反而比 come 更能顯出句意，故在這個子句裡副詞的內容性大於功能性，且比原本的內容字有更大的內容性。第二個子句的副詞 really，表示 sick 的程度，並不影響整個句意，所以這裡的副詞 really 功能性大於內容性。一般而言，表示程度的副詞如 very 或這裡的 really 都是功能性大而沒有內容性。

Part 2. 綜合範例

根據上述說明，分析句子中的內容字與功能字。（本範例中，畫底線的是內容字。）

◎ MP3 023

1 Though <u>Jack</u> was <u>poor</u> and <u>sick</u>, he never <u>gave up</u> any <u>chance</u> to <u>write</u>. That is <u>why</u> he finally <u>became</u> a <u>successful</u> <u>writer</u>. （96 年第二次基測）

（雖然 Jack 又窮又病，他絕不放棄任何能寫作的機會。這就是為什麼他最終成為一個成功作家的原因。）

首先，先將名詞動詞等內容字詞劃線，再看看其他形容詞副詞對句意是否有影響，判斷其是否內容性高。第一句話中的 Jack、gave up、chance、write 等內容字已經顯示出基本的句意，再看到 Be 動詞後的形容詞 poor 和 sick 內容性比較高故也劃線。第二句的 Be 動詞 is 沒有含意，屬功能性的字，所以內容性就落在它後面的疑問詞 why。become 雖然為動詞，是內容字，但它後面的形容詞 successful 也具有高度內容性影響句意，所以也可以劃線。

2 A: Oh, no! <u>I</u> <u>left</u> my <u>cell phone</u> on the <u>train</u>.
 B: <u>Let's</u> <u>call</u> the <u>station</u> and <u>ask</u> if <u>anyone</u> has <u>found</u> it. （95 年第一次基測）

（A: 喔！不好了！我把我的手機留在火車上了。B: 我們打電話到車站問問看有沒有任何人有找到它。）

先把主詞和動詞內容字劃線就已經可以看出句意。再來逐字分析，I 雖是代名詞，但在這裡代表主詞，所以也很重要。Let's 也是一樣的道理。

3 <u>House</u> <u>prices</u> are <u>dropping</u>, so you can <u>buy</u> a house at a <u>lower</u> price than before. （100 年第二次基測）

（房價下跌了，所以你能買到比之前低價的房子。）

⊘ drop（*v.*）下降、落下

⋯⋯⋯⋯⋯⋯⋯⋯⋯⋯⋯⋯⋯⋯⋯⋯⋯⋯⋯⋯⋯⋯⋯⋯⋯⋯

內容字多是名詞和動詞，在這句裡 house、price 和 dropping、buy 很明顯是內容字，第二次出現的 house 和 price 更加強調它的重要性，形容詞 lower 也能重複加強動詞 dropping 的含意。所以結合了這些字：房子、價錢、下降、買、更低，便能了解句子的主要意義。

4 <u>Three months</u> ago, <u>workers</u> frantically <u>tried to cool</u> <u>several</u> <u>reactors</u> at the <u>Fukushima Daiichi plant</u>, <u>225 kilometers</u> <u>north</u> of <u>Tokyo</u>. （改寫自 diegotaioli.wordpress.com）

（三個月前，工人們拼命地試著讓距離東京北方 225 公里的福島核電廠數個反應爐冷卻。）

⋯⋯⋯⋯⋯⋯⋯⋯⋯⋯⋯⋯⋯⋯⋯⋯⋯⋯⋯⋯⋯⋯⋯⋯⋯⋯

這句話裡幾乎都是內容字，因為在這句話裡有較多的資訊。一方面是跟數字有關的：three months、225 kilometers，有數字與名詞在一起時，該數字雖然是形容詞但具有重要性。動詞 tried 與 cool 都是內容字，但後者比較重要。專有名詞也是內容字，可能第一次聽會無法聽清楚，但只要先聽到聲音有個印象，之後如果是文章裡的重點就會不停出現，所以聽到專有名詞也不用太緊張。另外，這句的副詞 frantically（瘋狂地）用以形容 workers 努力的程度，並不會影響太多句意，所以只能算是功能性字詞。

【詳解請見 p206】

Part 3。練習題

分析句子中的內容字與功能字，並將能掌握句意的內容字劃線。

◎ MP3 **024**

① Why does your roommate think he should look for a cheaper apartment?

② I apologize for coming late to the meeting this morning.

③ The turtle is the animal my sister is most afraid of. She cries and runs away even when she sees a picture of one.（100 年第二次基測）

④ Nature can color our everyday lives with lovely surprises.
（100 年第二次基測）

⑤ Mom, thank you for everything you've done for Tim and me.
（99 年第一次基測）

⑥ Happy Puppy is a relatively new service.（96 年學測）

⑦ If you had listened carefully, this accident never would have happened.

⑧ This lecture will definitely produce an exciting debate.

⑨ Please exercise caution and read all safety instructions before use.

⑩ It is highly recommended for those who plan to go to graduate school.
（96 年學測）

⑪ Ms. Li's business expanded very quickly. (96 年學測)

⑫ As a health editor, I am often inundated by information about the latest disease, the newest cure, the healthiest diet, or the best exercise.

⑬ The young Taiwanese pianist performed remarkably well and won the first prize in the music competition. (97 年指考)

⑭ A: Can you see what the word is? The first letter is not clear.
　B: Oh, it's "r." The word is "ring." (95 年第一次基測)

⑮ A: Here's the order: Williams, Smith, Lewis, and Jones.
　　Yes, Lewis?
　B: I wan to go last.
　A: I've already decided. The sequence is fixed.

Lesson 5

否定字詞與助動詞

🔑 Part 1。 要訣：否定含意字詞的表達

一般來說，英文句中表示「不」的否定含意有三種表示方法：

一、Be 動詞 + not

二、助動詞 + not

三、使用具有否定含意的字詞，如 never、hardly 等。

第一和第二部分，需要注意的事項：

> ▶ 動詞是 Be 動詞或助動詞時，要表示否定含意，只需要在之後加上 not 即可。
>
> ▶ Be 動詞或助動詞加 not 時，通常會縮寫為一個字，除非要強調 not 時才會分開。
>
> ▶ 在聽的時候，要注意重音的改變，原本 Be 動詞或助動詞唸輕音，但加上 not 後就會變成重音。

Point 1 be 動詞 + not

◎ MP3 **025**

1 She **isn't** my cousin.

（她不是我的表姊。）

2 They **weren't** at the party last night.

（他們昨晚沒有到舞會。）

3 This book is **not** what I ordered.

（這本書不是我訂的。）

當想要強調 "not" 時，不跟前面 Be 動詞 is 連音，此時 is 仍為輕音，將重音在 not 上。

4 I'm <u>not</u> going to the museum with you.
（我沒有要跟你一起去博物館。）

當 not 沒有跟 Be 動詞連音時，像這句的 am 無法跟 not 連音，所以仍保持輕音，not 是重音。

Point 2 助動詞 + not

◎ MP3 026

助動詞包括 do/does、did、will、can、could、should、would、have/has、had 等等，加 not 的用法和注意事項跟前述的 Be 動詞相同。

1 I <u>don't</u> know!
（我不知道！）
2 Alice <u>didn't</u> answer my call.
（Alice 沒有回我電話。）
3 Kevin <u>hasn't</u> finished his work yet.
（Kevin 還沒有完成他的工作。）
4 He <u>couldn't</u> forget the night he met Judy.
（他無法忘記他和 Judy 相遇的那個晚上。）
5 David <u>can't</u> find his wallet.（91 年第一次基測）
（David 無法找到他的錢包。）

注意 can + not 在口語上會縮寫省略，變成 can't，並改變發音。但在寫作上，尤其是較正式的文章，不會縮寫而是寫成 cannot。

◎ MP3 **027**

　　所謂否定字詞就是除了 not 以外，含有否定含意的字，包括 no、never、nothing、few、little、seldom、rarely、hardly、barely、scarcely 等副詞。使用或聆聽這些否定含意的副詞有幾項需要注意的地方：

▶ 句子中有這些字詞時，都是直述句，不需要再加上 not 以免造成雙重否定而錯誤傳達語意。

▶ 口語上比較少用這種用法，大多出現在演講等比較正式的場合。

▶ 使用否定副詞時，常常會將之放到句首然後主詞動詞倒裝，在聆聽時必須特別注意這個字，因為是全句的重點。

1　I have no patience with kids.
（我對小孩沒有耐心。）

這句和 I don't have patience with kids. 相似，但使用否定字 no 在句中就用直述句，而不需再用 not 成否定句，仍然有否定的意思。而且更能強調完全沒有的程度。

2　I have little faith in the politics.
（我對政治沒什麼信心。）

little 含意上雖是小的、少的，但含有否定含意「幾乎沒有」的意思。

3　I will never do that again! = Never will I do that again.
（我絕不會再做那件事。）

有否定字詞的句子常會倒裝，用以強調該字否定的意思。這句若將 never 放句首就能明顯強調「決不」的意思。

Part2。綜合範例

聆聽 MP3 音檔，並根據以上原則注意標示出的否定字詞。

◎ MP3 028

1 It <u>isn't</u> a good way to learn a foreign language.

（這不是一個學習外語的好方法。）

一般 not 都會跟前面 be 動詞連音，注意連音後這個縮寫字就會發重音，強調出否定含意。

2 If we go north or south, we <u>won't</u> notice any difference, because there is usually <u>no</u> time zone change.（94 年學測）

（如果我們往北或南走，我們將不會注意到任何差異，因為沒有時差。）

這句的兩個否定字，will not 縮寫成 won't，唸法也會隨之改變，也會從輕音變重音。第二個否定字 no 不縮寫，以肯定句呈現，也是用重音強調「沒有」。

3 Things you've <u>never</u> seen during the daytime are all here waiting to say hi to you at night.（改寫自 92 年第一次基測）

（你從沒有在白天看過的景物，晚上全都在這裡等著跟你打招呼。）

使用否定字詞都是用肯定句來表達，也不跟其他字連音或縮寫，而且一定發重音來強調其否定含意。

4 Jo likes summer <u>the least</u> because she has serious problems sleeping in the summer heat.（100 年第二次基測）

（Jo 最不喜歡夏天因為她很困難於在夏日炎熱中入眠。）

the least 最少的，也是含有負面含意的字，所以用直述句就可以表示否定含意，即 Jo 最不喜歡夏天。

5 **I <u>can't</u> find my history book, but I know it's somewhere in the living room.**（100 年第一次基測）

（我找不到我的歷史書，但我知道它就在客廳的某個地方。）

助動詞 can + not 在口語上是 can't，必須注意它的縮寫念法比較特別，發 kant。

【詳解請見 p208】

聆聽 **MP3** 音檔，寫出句子中的否定字詞。

◎ MP3 **029**

❶ I _____ mean to hurt you.

❷ She _____ received my letter yet.

❸ After all, machines _____ be more important than people.
（91 年第二次基測）

❹ I'm _____ sure whether we can still go fishing tomorrow.
（92 年第二次基測）

❺ I have _____ interest in cooking, so I always ask my brother
to cook for me.（92 年第二次基測）

❻ I _____ imagine that there were fish in the water before.
（91 年第二次基測）

❼ I see _____ but sand.

❽ Sandy _____ gets up before 8 a.m.

❾ Although he is a chef, Roberto _____ cooks his own meals.
（94 年學測）

❿ He is too busy and can _____ have dinner with his family.

⓫ Badly injured in the car accident, Jason could _____ move his legs and was sent to the hospital right away. (99 年學測)

⑫ This animal is _____ seen because it lives 4,000 meters under the sea and is hard to find. (改寫自 100 年第一次基測)

⑬ _____ you do that! _____ you say your good-byes! (電影 *Titanic* 鐵達尼號)

⑭ If he'd told me before he did it, I _____ be so angry now.

⑮ Although that chemistry experiment they were doing _____ difficult, they _____ able to get any useful data.

Lesson 6
句子的節奏與音調

🔑 Part 1。 要訣：掌握節奏和音調

根據每個人說話的不同習慣，在講述英文句子時也會有不同的節奏與音調。但即使如此，我們還是可以找出一些大原則以便輕鬆的掌握說話者的句意。

一、節奏：因人而異，但主要依停頓原則
二、音調：A. 肯定句下沉
    B. 否定句先上升再下沉
    C. 疑問句上揚

Point 1　節奏

◎ MP3 **030**

有的人話說得很快不需要停頓休息，節奏自然就很快。但也有人說話非常慢。但一般而言，講英文句子會依照一定的習慣而稍作停頓，所以聆聽長句子尤其可以發現這些原則的運用。一般習慣是會在連接詞及片語之前稍做休息換氣，或是看句子的結構來分段。（詳細原則請看 Lesson 1 停頓）

1 The boys are now 25 years old / and will come back home / for the first time / since they left ten years ago. （94 年第二次基測）
（這些男孩們如今已經 25 歲，將會在離開十年後第一次回到家鄉。）

子句 / 連接詞 and / 片語 for the first time / 時間子句

技巧篇

句子很長時，任何人在說的時候都可能需要停下來換氣，依據停頓的原則，這句可以分三段，或許不是每個人都會節奏一樣，但至少會在其中停一至兩次。

2 Some simple strategies can help / even the pickiest eater / learn to like a more varied diet.（98 年學測）

（一些簡單的策略甚至可以幫助最挑食的人去學著喜歡更多樣化的飲食。）

- ☑ strategy（*n.*）戰略　☑ picky（*adj.*）挑剔的
- ☑ varied（*adj.*）多樣的　☑ diet（*n.*）飲食

這句話中沒有連接詞或子句來做明顯分段，但根據文法結構仍然可以分為三段。在受詞 even the pickiest eater 前後分段。說話快的人可能不需分段，但一般人可能會選擇在其中停頓一次。

Point 2 音調

◎ MP3 **031**

說話音調也是會因人而異，加上遇到內容字又會加重音，所以音調會起起伏伏，但大方向來看，肯定句會往下降，疑問句會上揚，而否定句會比肯定句多一個起伏再往下降。所以以下用這三種類型不同的句子來討論：

A. 肯定句

肯定句句尾音調都會下沉，但如果句子太長，前面的子句會在節奏分段的地方先往上揚，然後再往下。

1 The fire in the fireworks factory in Changhua / set off a series of powerful explosions / and killed four people.（94 年學測）

（位於彰化爆竹工廠的這場火引發一連串嚴重的爆炸並奪走了四條人命。）

依文法原則，這句話可以分為三小段，在每個分段點可能停頓一下，音調語氣也可能會微微上揚，然後在最後一段音調往下。

2 I am studying so hard for the upcoming entrance exam / that I do not have the luxury of a free weekend to rest. （95 年學測）
（我正爲了即將來臨的入學考試非常努力唸書，以至於無法奢侈地休息一個周末。）

☑ luxury（*n.*）奢侈

長一點的句子，雖然不會在每一個文法分段點都停頓或音調上揚，但總是會需要休息，此句最明顯需要停頓處是兩個子句中間，然後在第二個子句再下沉。

技巧篇

B. 否定句

跟肯定句相同，否定句的句尾語氣也會下降。但不同的是，否定句在說到否定含義字詞的時候，會先往上再落下以表示強調語氣，之後再往上回到原來的音調。也就是說，否定句會比肯定句多一個起伏在否定字上。

3 I just can't picture you tap dancing.
（我只是無法想像你跳踢踏舞。）

在這句短句中，在說 can't 這個否定字時音調往上並加重音，然後再回到直述句的下墜語氣。

4 I was not home when the mail carrier brought the package, so I'll have to get it myself at the post office. （97 年第一次基測）
（郵差送包裏來時我不在家，所以我必須自己去郵局拿。）

和肯定句相同，此句會在 so 之前的子句先音調上揚，在第二個子句再下降。但說到 not 這個否定字時，會先往上，說完再往下。所以多了一個 not，這句話就比沒有 not 多了一個起伏。

C. 疑問句

表示疑問的句子的語氣一般是會往上揚，但根據不同的問法，會有不同的語調，這部分會在下一章節詳細說明。

5　How can you study in the living room / when other people are watching TV?（99 年第一次基測）
（你怎麼能在客廳唸書當其他人都在那看電視？）

不是每種問句都會明顯上揚的音調，這句以 how 為首的問句就不會上揚，而在疑問字 how 上加重語氣。

6　If you are so good, / why don't you want to help other people to do it?（98 年第二次基測）
（如果你是個很好的球員，你會想要幫助其他人練習嗎？）

以 why 為首的問句不上揚，而在 why 上加重語氣。

注意！這章節所談到的節奏和音調跟前面的章節有雷同之處，大方向而言是相同的，但較強調個人講話的速度。本章主要針對的是比較長的句子。長一點的句子會因為個人習慣不同而有落差，尤其是說話者的口音與說話速度。再者，長句會因為節奏更多而導致語調也起伏更多。

Part 2 ▸ 綜合範例

聆聽 MP3 音檔，並根據以上原則注意標示出的音調與節奏。

◎ MP3 032

1 **Larry, / my American friend in Taiwan, / has learned to use chopsticks well / and can eat beef noodles / the way most Taiwanese people do.** （98 年第二次基測）

（我在台灣的美國朋友 Larry 學習使用筷子，他學得很好，並可以像大多數台灣人 一樣吃牛肉麵。）

✓ chopsticks（*n.*）筷子

先試著將長句分段以感覺句子的節奏，雖然節奏可能會因為每個人說話的快慢呼吸有所不同。仔細聽 MP3，找出說話者的節奏分段，再來分析語句的音調，這句話是肯定句，句尾語氣下沉，但長句時中間會先上揚，以這句為例，可以連接詞 and 為分段點先語氣上揚，到句尾再下沉。

2 **Are you interested in playing basketball / but have never had the chance to play it?** （98 年第二次基測）

（你曾經對打籃球有興趣卻從沒機會打過？）

一般是非問句的音調在字尾要上揚，但句子若長一些，在中間分段點如此句的連接詞 but，音調可先微微下降，再上揚。

3 **Sing to nature's music, / dance with the wind, / and look for the magic of life.** （100 年第二次基測）

（跟著大自然的音韻而唱，隨著風舞動，找尋生命的魔力。）

這句話按逗點可分三個小段，每段的結構也很類似，都是【動詞＋介系詞＋受詞】。動詞重音，介系詞輕音，受詞再加一點重音。多聽多唸，感受這句像詩一般的語調節奏。

4 **How** much money / did your boss raise / at the fundraiser / for the orphanage / last week?

（你老闆上星期為孤兒院的募款活動募到多少錢？）
☑ raise（*v.*）募款　☑ fundraiser（*n.*）籌募資金活動
☑ orphanage（*n.*）孤兒院

這個問句尾音不上揚，而是平穩下降，原因請看下一章。How much 是詢問的重點，所以 how 要加重音，另外按照結構分段。原本片語 for the orphanage 之前或片語 at the fundraiser 之前都會停頓，但其實口語不會每個停頓點都停，會依個人習慣和速度改變，所以聆聽 MP3 中的發音語調，多念並找出自己的速度跟節奏。

5 **When you hear birds singing, / do you want to sing with them? / When the light winds blows, / can you feel it's friendly touch on your face? / Are you excited to see the first little flower in the early spring?**（100 第二次基測）

（當你聽到鳥兒歌唱，你會想要跟著它們唱嗎？當清爽的風吹著，你會感覺在你臉上它那友善的觸摸嗎？目睹早春第一朵的小花，你會感到興奮嗎？）

這裡連三個是非疑問句語氣明顯上揚，前兩句都是 when 加重音並接子句微微下降的音調，在問句時再往上揚。結構相似的語句並排，又是上揚的音調，可以感覺出說話者的情緒漸漸高漲，像在往上爬樓梯一般。用以突顯最後一句問句中的 excited 興奮這個字和情緒。斷句停頓跟著逗點、句點與結構，但最後一句因為顯示興奮心情可能不會停頓，快速唸完並語調上升。

Part 3. 練習題 【詳解請見 p208】

聆聽句子後，試著找出說話者的節奏與語調，將句子劃斜線分出節奏並劃出上升或下降的音調。而且，請務必跟著一起念出聲來。

◎ MP3 033

❶ Cheese, powdered milk, and yogurt are common milk products.
（94 年學測）

❷ We are completely devoted to helping dogs enjoy a full and active life.
（96 年學測）

❸ This new computer is obviously superior to the old one because it has many new functions. （97 年學測）

❹ Sally, a junior high school student, would like to go to the Big Dream Summer Camp. （98 年第二次基測）

❺ Do you have all your figures ready for the auditors who are coming in?

❻ Did you get into trouble for getting home late from our date?

❼ Under the leadership of newly elected president Barack Obama, the US is expected to turn a new page in its history.

❽ I really don't believe that Kevin can complete the job, even with the help of the new assistant.

❾ Because of the high levels of air pollution, officials decided it was not the right time to reduce the vehicle tax.

⑩ To live an efficient life, we have to arrange the things to do in order of priority and start with the most important ones.（94 學測）

⑪ She was about to call 911 again when the intruder managed to stand up, with David clinging to his back.

⑫ According to many observers, the Hollywood movie star George Clooney played a pivotal role in Sudan's historic referendum.

⑬ What was most touching and encouraging for me was to see farmers, even beggars donating and doing their part.

⑭ Most Americans believe that human trafficking happens everywhere but in their country.

⑮ Twisted every way, what answer can I give? Am I to risk my life to win the chance to live? Can I betray the man who once inspired my voice? Do I become his prey? Do I have any choice?（電影 *The Phantom of the Opera* 歌劇魅影）

Lesson 7

問句

🔑 Part 1. 要訣：不同疑問句的語調

英文的問句可以分為很多種類型，因為不同的類型，語調也會不同。以下將問句分為五種：

一、是非疑問句
二、疑問詞疑問句（訊息疑問句）
三、否定疑問句
四、附加問句
五、非疑問的問句（問句型式，但非詢問他人意見）

Point 1　是非疑問句

◎ MP3 034

是非疑問句是將 Be 動詞或助動詞放在句首表示，而且語調在句尾會有明顯上揚。如例句 1、2、3。表示禮貌的詢問也常用這種方式，如例句 4。另外，非正式的口語也常會將主詞和助動詞省略簡化詢問，如例句 5、6。這類型的問句音調上都會在句尾明顯上揚。

1 Is everything going well?
（一切都好嗎？）

2 Have you finished using the photocopier?
(Are you done with the copier?)
（你使用完影印機了嗎？）

3 Do you think we should hire a new secretary to replace Julia?

（你認為我們應該請一個新祕書來取代 Julia 嗎？）

以上三句都是用 Be 動詞及一般助動詞為句首的是非疑問句，所以很明顯可以感覺到句尾上升的音調。

4 Would you pass me that book, please?

（請把那本書拿給我好嗎？）

這類型問句也可使用 would、could 等情態助動詞來表示禮貌的詢問。

5 Finish your work?

（完成你的工作了嗎？）

非正式的口語常將這類型的問句省略前面的 Be 動詞或助動詞以及主詞。如這句原句可能是 Did you finish your work? 然後省略 did you 而成。省略後的問句，其音調仍是明顯上揚。

6 Anything else?

（還有其他的嗎？）

這個疑問句省略了更多，可能是 Is there anything else? 或 Do you want anything else? 都有可能。

Point 2 疑問詞疑問句（訊息疑問句）

◎ MP3 035

將疑問詞放句首的問句就是疑問詞疑問句。疑問詞包括 who、

where、when、why、what、which、how，或其他像 whose，whom，how many，how much 等等。這類型問句的答句就不可能只是 yes 或 no，而是想要詢問某些特定資訊，故也稱為訊息疑問句。這種問句的音調不會在句尾上揚，反而是會往下墜。疑問詞通常會加重音強調，音調會先上揚一些然後在句尾又會下墜。

1 What happened?
（發生什麼事？）

句子因為很短，可以明顯聽下沉的語調。

2 Why is this announcement being made at this time?
（為什麼在此刻發出這個通知？）

3 How much does the conference cost?
（這個研討會要花多少錢？）

4 Where is the best place to get a business loan these days?
（目前去哪裡申請商業貸款最好呢？）

5 Who wanted to have publicly supported universities?
（誰想要設立公立大學？）

Point 3 否定疑問句

◎ MP3 036

這類型的問句和第一種的是非疑問句幾乎相同，只是在句首的 Be 動詞或助動詞加上 not，用否定的口氣詢問。音調上也是在句尾上揚。回答這種否定疑問句的方式也和是非疑問句相同。此外，因為這兩種問句其實有一樣的效果，口語上仍是習慣使用單純的是非疑問句。

1 Didn't he accept this reason?

（他沒有接受這個理由嗎？）

2 Aren't we supposed to have a meeting at three o'clock?

（我們三點不是要開會嗎？）

3 Don't you agree that Tom has all the necessary experience for this position?

（難道你不同意 Tom 具備了這個職位所必需的經驗嗎？）

4 Doesn't she live in the dormitory?

（她不是住在宿舍嗎？）

Point 4 附加問句

◎ MP3 037

這種問句是在前面的直述句後，加上助動詞或 Be 動詞以及主詞的代名詞用反面含意來詢問。這種問句表示詢問者已經幾乎確定答案而只是要再度確認。音調上，前面的直述句語氣下沉，但在後面簡短的附加問句音調就要立刻上揚。

1 Everything is okay, isn't it?

（每件事都順利，對吧？）

附加問句的 Be 動詞或助動詞會跟前面直述句的相反，如這句的直述句是用 is，那麼附加問句就會是 isn't。而且注意在附加問句時都是用代名詞代替主詞。

2 They aren't your books, are they?

（他們不是你的書，對吧？）

如果前面的直述句是否定的 Be 動詞或助動詞，後面接的附加問句就是肯定的，反之亦然。

3 He has learned a lot in the last couple of years, hasn't he?

（他在過去這些年已經學了很多，對吧？）

Point 5 非疑問的問句

◎ MP3 038

　　非疑問的問句意思是句子表面上看起來像是詢問，但事實上說話者已經有答案並且不期待對方有回應。說話者使用這種疑問句其實是要引發聽者去思考以強調這句話中的意義或是表現出諷刺的意味。

1 Who do you think you are?

（你以為你是誰？）

....

此句只是要提醒聽者注意自己的身分而不是真的要問聽者的姓名或身分。

2 What has he ever done for me?

（他有為我做過什麼嗎？）

....

這句話雖然是問 what，但其實是要強調讓聽者知道 he 並沒有為 me 做過什麼事。

3 How much longer do our people have to endure this injustice?

（我們人民要忍受多久這種不公平？）

☑ endure（*v.*）忍受　☑ injustice（*n.*）不公正

Part 2. 綜合範例

仔細聆聽並跟著唸，注意這些問句的音調起伏。

◎ MP3 039

1 Are you going to wear a suit to the seminar tomorrow?

（明天的討論會你會穿西裝嗎？）

☑ suit（*n.*）西裝　☑ seminar（*n.*）研討會

....

這句是是非疑問句，所以注意句尾音調要上揚。

2 Where were they going after the seminar?

（討論會後他們去了哪裡？）

....

疑問詞為句首的問句就是訊息疑問句，根據上面所說的原則，本句音調不會在句尾往上，而是先會往上，句尾再往下。

3 Is the dog that bites people yours? You should keep it home.（100 年第一次基測）

（這隻咬人的狗是你的嗎？你應該要把它關在家裡。）

....

此問句看起來是簡單的是非疑問句，但後面的句子顯示問的人其實已經知道答案而進一步的譴責，所以這個問句可以算是非疑問的問句，語氣上因為形式是是非疑問句所以仍然要語氣往上揚，但口氣上跟純粹的疑問有差別。

4 How about coffee, drinks, dinner, or a movie, for as long as we both shall live?（電影 *You've Got Mail* 電子情書）

（要不要一起去喝杯咖啡、喝點小酒、吃個晚餐、還是看場電影，只要我們彼此都還活著？）

這是疑問詞開頭的疑問句但不是問程度 how 而是提議 how about 的問句，所以除了 how 加重音，在 how about 後的各項建議也要上揚。

5 **How** can you forgive this guy for standing you up and not forgiving me for this tiny little thing like putting you out of business?（電影 *You've Got Mail* 電子情書）

（你怎麼能原諒那個讓你空等的傢伙卻不能為了這一點小小的事原諒我，我不過就是讓你沒了工作？）

　stand ... up（*ph.*）放……鴿子

這句 How 開頭的疑問詞疑問句，how 要加重音，句子雖然有點長，但整體而言仍是往下降的。另外，這句很明顯的是屬於上述分類問句的第五種，非疑問的問句，主要不是要表示懷疑而是想要使聽者去思考句子含意，並不算是個問句。這種非疑問性的問句外表形式都和一般問句相同，語調規則也是和一般問句一樣，主要是必須看整體對話或上下文情境才感覺得出來。

Part 3. 練習題

仔細聆聽並跟著唸，注意這些問句的音調起伏並在句子上畫出線條。

◎ MP3 **040**

1. Are you alright?

2. She didn't attend the meeting, did she?

3. What service does this company offer?

4. Aren't you supposed to be in class now?

5. Do you mind my smoking here?

6. When will Tom be able to complete this project?

7. Is it true you put in for a transfer to London?

8. Would you like to go swimming with me?

9. How do these people feel about the television sets?

10. Why are you so stupid?

11. Could you give me a hand?

12. Could you leave the door open a little, Sarah?

技巧篇

⑬ What is the main purpose of the announcement?

⑭ Henry, don't you think fishing is boring? You just sit by the water and wait all day long.（100 年第一次基測）

⑮ A: Based on the weather report, when will sun rise?
   B: You've asked me more than ten times. Be patient, okay?

Lesson 8

資訊的重點

🔑 Part 1.
要訣：快速掌握句子的語意重點

　　根據先前的原則，我們可以藉由字詞輕重、語調節奏等原則了解英文句子的含義。但在了解句意之外，必須進一步學習如何快速抓到句子所要表達的語意重點。一般來說，資訊的重點都放在主詞與動詞，掌握這兩類字詞，就很容易掌握語意。如一般英文聽力測驗，不論是大考、多益或全民英檢，主要都是要進行這類的練習。

　　以下可分為兩種情形分析：

一、講述背景：包括 5W1H（人物、時間、地點、事物、原因、方式）等資訊

二、敘述因果：含有原因或結果含意的字詞或句子

Point 1　講述背景

◎ MP3 **041**

　　訓練掌握句子重點的第一步，是要能把握 5W1H 的資訊（who 人、where 地點、what 事物、when 時間、why 原因以及 how 如何）。一般在講述事件時，這些基本的背景資料要能聽清楚，才能做更進一步的其他分析。

1 **Betty goes jogging every day in the park, and Allen does, too.**
（97 年第一次基測）
（Betty 每天在公園裡慢跑，Allen 也是。）

在這個短句中所提供的背景資料有：goes jogging 慢跑（what）、every day 每天（when）、in the park 公園裡（where）以及 Allen（who）。捉住每個背景資訊後再依後面文句取出重點。

2 Michael Phelps, an American swimmer, broke seven world records and won eight gold medals in men's swimming contests in the 2008 Olympics.（99 年學測）
（Michael Phelps 是美國泳者，他打破 7 項世界紀錄並在 2008 年奧林匹克贏得 8 面男子泳賽金牌。）
⊘ medal（*n.*）獎章　⊘ Olympics（*n.*）奧林匹克運動會

注意在聽取句中資訊重點時，主詞通常不是重點，介系詞也可以不用太注意，主要是先設想這句話說者可能想要表達的事。這句話就可能會把重點放在 Michael Phelps 的成就（what）：broke seven world records 和 won eight gold medals，尤其遇到數字時又更需要注意一下。次要的重點可能會在 American 或 2008 Olympics 及 swimming。

3 A: Let's go for a walk.
B: Okay, let me change into shorts though.
A: Could you get my sunglasses from the bedroom?
（A: 我們去散步吧！ B: 好，讓我先去換個短褲。 A: 能幫我從臥室拿我的太陽眼鏡嗎？）

對話中因為句子短，重點比較容易掌握，但要注意單字中延伸的含義。可以預測次要重點在 walk 散步（what）或 bedroom 臥室（where），但更明顯的重點是 shorts 短褲以及 sunglasses 太陽眼鏡所代表的意思，即外面是豔陽高照的好天氣。

◎ MP3 **042**

　　找出背景資料是訓練掌握資訊的第一步，但有時背景資訊太多且也不見得是文句的重點，其實重點不一定落在某些字詞上，而是要了解句意後找到前後因果關係才是語句想要表達的重點。

1 Due to inflation, prices for daily necessities have gone up and we have to pay more for the same items now. (99 年學測)

（因為通貨膨脹，生活必需品的價格上升，同樣的物品我們現在必須付更多的錢。）

☑ inflation（*n.*）通貨膨脹　☑ daily necessities（*n.*）日常生活用品

本句的因果關係很明顯，原因是 inflation 通貨膨脹，所造成的結果是 price up 價格上升，pay more 付出更多。

2 Football is more than a sport; it is also a teacher. In teaching players to cooperate with their fellows on the field, the game shows them the necessity of teamwork in society.

（足球不只是個運動，它也是個老師。教導球員在球場上與同伴合作時，就展現了社會中團隊運作的必要性。）

☑ cooperate（*v.*）合作

聽長句的時候，資訊的重點不會只在一兩個字上，必須注意前因後果。第一句先說結論，下一句就解釋原因，把握住原因就是這段話的重點。後面提到的重點字有 cooperate 以及 teamwork，這些字便可以解釋足球為何是個老師的原因。

Part 2. 範例

練習找出句子中的資訊，第一步可以將背景資訊找出並畫線，如果有很多資訊時，試著找出最重要的重點，通常是含有因果關係的字句。最後可用自己的話說出該段的重點。

MP3 043

1 My name is <u>Mark Lin</u>. I was born on <u>September 1, 1981</u>. I enjoy <u>music and movies</u> a lot, and <u>swimming</u> is my favorite sport. Since I finished school, I <u>have worked for six years</u> at <u>my parents' farm</u>. I hope I can <u>have my own business</u> soon.

（97 年第一次基測）

（我的名字是 Mark Lin。我出生於 1981 年 9 月 1 日。我很喜歡音樂和電影，而游泳是我最喜歡的運動。自從我結束學校生活，我在我父母的農場工作已經 6 年，我希望我能很快擁有自己的事業。）

這段主要講述 Mark 的生日、興趣、工作與未來期許。根據 5W1H 的原則很容易可以找出背景的資訊。雖然這段話只是背景描述，所以都是背景的資訊，但若還有下文描述這個角色的故事，那麼就可進一步知道哪一個資訊最重要。

2 Native Americans could not understand the white men's war on the <u>wolf</u>. The Indians considered the <u>wolf their spiritual brother</u>. <u>They respected the animal's hunting ability, and warriors prayed to hunt like wolves.</u>

（美國原住民不能了解白人對狼的爭鬥。印第安人認為狼是他們精神上的弟兄。他們尊敬這動物的狩獵能力，勇士們並祈禱自己能狩獵得像狼一樣。）

☑ native（*adj.*）本國的　☑ spiritual（*adj.*）精神上的　☑ warrior（*n.*）戰士

重點在於印地安人對狼的尊重與欽慕。這段敘述沒有明顯的背景資訊可以掌握，但由於 wolf 重複出現，我們可以判定為重要資訊。第二次出現時 their spiritual brothers 跟隨在後提供我們更多線索。最後一句沒有明顯的重點字但整句都在解釋原因，故也是最重要的資訊。

3 **A census taker once <u>tried to test me</u>. <u>I ate his liver</u> with some fava beans and a nice Chianti.**

（電影 *The Silence of the Lambs* 沉默的羔羊）

（有個調查人員有一次想試驗我，我把他的肝伴著蠶豆配 Chianti 酒吃了。）
☑census（*n.*）人口普查、調查　☑liver（*n.*）肝　☑fava beans（*n.*）蠶豆

重點在於說話者討厭被人測試以及他會吃人肉。這句電影的台詞中，若配合影像會更容易抓到重點，光聽句子的話，只要聽懂動詞跟主受詞就能了解其中因果關係。前一句是某人（主詞沒聽懂沒關係，只要知道是個人即可），動作是 try to test，受詞 me。而下一句馬上接主詞 I，動詞 ate ，以及受詞 his liver。兩句相連馬上能感受到句中要表達的驚悚感。

4 **Police have identified the <u>suspect</u> as <u>Behring Breivik</u>, 32, a suspected <u>right-wing Christian extremist</u> who seems to have written a <u>1,500-page manifesto</u> ranting <u>against Muslims</u> and laying out meticulous plans to prepare for the <u>attacks</u> without being detected.**

（摘錄自 http://politicsandpeople.org/tag/nancy-pelosi/）

（警方指認出一名叫 Behring Breivik 的 32 歲嫌犯，他是個右派基督教狂熱分子，他似乎寫了 1,500 頁的宣言斥罵回教徒，並且展示他精心策劃不被發現的攻擊計畫。）
☑suspect（*n.*）嫌疑犯　☑right-wing（*adj.*）右派的　☑Christian（*n.*）基督教的

⊘extremist（*n.*）極端份子　⊘manifesto（n.）宣言　⊘rant（*v.*）怒氣沖沖的叫喊
⊘Muslim（*n.*）回教　⊘lay out（*ph.*）展示　⊘meticulous（*adj.*）小心翼翼的
⊘attack（*v.*）攻擊　⊘detect（*v.*）偵查

此段重點在於嫌疑犯的資料以及初步犯案原因。這類像新聞報導的句子最容易會有很多背景的資訊，尤其是專有名詞，一下子記不住也不要急，先記住音，大概拼出雛形即可，因為事後都能在書面上找到詳細資料，如這裡的 Anthony Breivik、38 歲或 1,500 頁的宣言。但 suspect 嫌疑犯這個字出現兩次，可見它很重要。聽懂 suspect 就能聯想到一些罪刑的單字，那麼接下來出現的 attacks（攻擊）就不難抓住。攻擊什麼呢？中間可能無法全部聽懂，若有聽到 right-wing 右派、Christians 基督教徒或 Muslims 回教徒之中的其中一個，就能猜出是和宗教信仰有關的攻擊事件。憑著聽到的名詞、動詞、關鍵字，慢慢就能拼出事件的雛形。

技巧篇

Part 3. 練習題 【詳解請見 p211】

找出句子中的資訊，第一步可以將背景資訊找出並畫線，如果有很多資訊時，試著找出最重要的重點，通常是含有因果關係的字句。最後可用自己的話說出該段的重點。

◎ MP3 044

❶ Many people like to drink bottled water because they feel that tap water may not be safe, but is bottled water really any better? (99 年學測)

❷ If the weather is fine this weekend, my family will go to the beach for three days.

❸ A: How about going to the cafeteria?
   B: It's too crowded.

❹ The islands have an average temperature of 80 degrees, so don't forget your shorts and swimsuits.

❺ A: Excuse me, when are the departures for Chicago today?
   B: Nine and ten o'clock, twelve- fifteen, two forty-five, and four-thirty.

❻ Due to poor weather conditions, all flights departing for New York will be postponed until further notice.

❼ Scientists discovered that eating plenty of pizza seems to lower the risk of cancer. The protective ingredient is tomato sauce.

❽ The annual Comic-Con conference is becoming more well-known as more major motion pictures are being based on comic book properties.

⑨ In television, the cancelled show is a common thing. Audience tastes are hard to predict, so every network is bound to produce its share of losers as well as winners.

⑩ When it gets hot outside, everyone starts obsessing over ice cream sandwiches. Not me. Instead, I want to talk about savory, greasy, fried grilled cheese sandwiches.

情境練習篇

Listening

Listening

情境練習篇前言

　　情境教學是最近較常見的練習方式，早期稱為 Situational Learning，強調以口語以及規則的練習，訓練的方式是會練習一些基本對話。90 年代後 Situated Learning 盛行，是將重點放在場景中，創造可能的情境，以及情境中常出現的狀況、用字、或語句，在情境中創造語言學習的材料，再去做溝通與活用。主要是在溝通中學習，而不像以往用制式化的對話練習。例如現實生活中打招呼的方式絕不可能制式化的總是問 How are you? 而且生活化的回答也不可能只有 I am fine, and you? 舊式的練習很明顯的不符合現實生活。情境教學中重要的是溝通，而非學英文。

　　生活中可能遇見的情形非常多，在本篇中略分為十一種情形，分析在某種情境中可能出現的工作狀況，並介紹這些工作狀況中使用的語言形式（包括慣用的表達方式與字詞用法）。例如廣告或新聞中的英文單字非常多，但常用的表達方式其實並不複雜。熟悉其表達的方式就能快速了解語句中的含意，即使根據不同事件會有一些變化，或是在實際情況下因不同人而有不同的口音，這些變動的因素都不會干擾太多，因為聽者在聆聽前就對內容以及表達方式有一定的理解與期待，不容易因少數變動而驚慌以致錯失重要的資訊。

　　接下來各章節所提供的範例也不是要去背的既定模式，而是要熟悉大略的期望字詞。同樣的，也強烈建議聽者不僅要聽也要唸出來。聽力其實跟口語是同時連貫的，再加上先前技巧篇的理解與練習，英文聽力一定會進步。

Lesson 9

描述

Part 1。
要訣：把握不同對象的描述重點

　　一般在描述時，會因為對象不同而有不同的重點。在這裡我們可以分為三種不同的對象：描述人物、描述物品以及描述景色。

Point 1　人物

◎ MP3 **045**

　　通常描述人物時會有的重點有以下幾項：人物姓名、工作職業、外表描述，以及個性特色。另外，新聞類的報導也會附加年齡。最後，都會有對於該人物的評論或對他的貢獻提出結論。

1 The winner of this year's award, Nay Phone Latt, a skinny 29-year-old man, is the voice of a new generation of Burmese who are finding ways around the authoritarian regime's censorship.
（今年的得獎者是 Nay Phone Latt，29 歲的男性，他是緬甸新世代之聲，在獨裁政權之下尋找可行之路。）

　　不要怕聽到一些不認識的字，捉住重點便能了解大概的含意。首先，主要描述人物的名字 Nay Phone Latt 並不好記，但是之後便有同位語描述他的外表特徵 skinny 以及年齡相關資訊 29-year-old man。第一句介紹他的話中還包括 a new generation of Burmese 可以知道他是個緬甸的新一代年輕人。最後一句可以讓聽者了解他的貢獻是在獨裁政權下尋找新出路。

　　對物品的描述著重在其尺寸大小、顏色及功能上的特色，所以在聽物品，尤其是商品的描述時，需要對數字特別敏感。

1　The Samsung AQ100 is a waterproof digital camera. It has a slim 0.8-inch thick body, and can be waterproof up to depths of 10 feet. The Aqua scene mode of Samsung AQ100 can take the best underwater photos. （改寫自 http://www.imaging-resource.com）
（Samsung AQ100 是防水數位相機。機身為輕薄的 0.8 吋厚度，可防水到 10 呎深度。Samsung AQ100 的水中影像模式能拍攝最佳的水中照片。）
　⊘ waterproof（*adj.*）防水的　　⊘ digital camera（*n.*）數位相機
　⊘ slim（*adj.*）苗條的　　⊘ aqua（*n.*）水

介紹物件的描述邏輯是最清楚明白的，先是名稱，再來是大小及相關的功能數值，如果有更需要強調的功能會再清楚介紹。這個範例 Samsung 牌型號 AQ100 號防水數位相機在一開始便會說明它的名稱及功能。另外，防水功能是主要強調的重點，所以會不停的重複，如 Aqua scene mode, underwater photography 等等。

　　對景色的描述，最重要的是會運用到視覺上的字眼來建構聽者腦中的畫面。最容易出現的視覺性字眼就是顏色，所以在聆聽景色相關的描述要先有對顏色字的了解。另外，因為和視覺有關，描述景色時大都符合人對

情境篇

視覺上的邏輯；例如可能會先有一個主題句給予聽者大方向的理解，再從左到右、從上到下、從近到遠的描述景物。

1 On the rough slopes of the remnants of St. Tila's main settlement, dry stone walls girdle the old houses. These beehive-shaped buildings with turf roofs are still undamaged.

（在草石遍佈的斜坡上是 Tila 山主要的居住地遺跡。乾砌的牆圍繞著老舊的小屋，這些蜂巢形狀的建築，以及其用草皮覆蓋的屋頂，都仍然完好無損。）

☑ slope（*n.*）傾斜、坡度　☑ remnant（*n.*）殘骸、遺跡

☑ girdle（*v.*）環繞　☑ turf（n.）草皮

第一句先給聽者大環境的概念，這裡這是山上的遺跡。鏡頭再往前進到外圍城牆 dry stone walls，然後再進到裡面的蜂巢型建築物 beehive-shaped buildings，接著看得更近一些到覆蓋草皮的屋頂 turf roofs。這是一個由外到內的景觀描述，雖然沒有顏色的形容，但仍有許多視覺相關的形狀或質感描述，如 rough slopes 草石遍佈的斜坡以及 beehive-shaped buildings 蜂巢形的建築等。

以上三種對象的描述，聽者可能會覺得對專有名詞的部分最難掌握，但其實在實際情境下，專有名詞都會有平面紙本的呈現，如名片或宣傳單等等。在任何資料都沒有提供的情形下，聽者也可以訓練用聽音節的方式寫下大略的字母做紀錄。主要是能把握對不同對象的描述重點，就能掌握到關鍵的訊息。

Part 2. 綜合範例

1 **Georgia O'Keeffe** was, starting in the <u>1920s</u>, a major figure in <u>American art</u>. She is chiefly known for <u>paintings of flowers, rocks, shells, animal bones, and landscapes</u>. She received widespread recognition for her <u>technical contributions and her modern style</u>. (改寫自 http://www.facebook.com/media/set/?set=a.1 87386771293714.44249.118346868197705&type=1)

（Georgia O'Keeffe 是美國藝術界 1920 年代起的主要人物。她主要以繪畫花朵、石頭、獸骨、貝殼與大地景物著名。她的工藝技術貢獻以及現代風格得到廣泛的認同。）

☑landscape（*n.*）風景　☑widespread（*adj.*）分布廣的
☑recognition（*n.*）認識、認可

描述人物的第一句通常就會將人物的名字提出，即使專有名字不好記，也可以先聽出音節有個大略的印象。出現名字之後會有相關的客觀描述，這段描述沒有外表描述但提供了 1920s 一個時代的資訊，並且也在第一句裡就提供了關於她的主要貢獻，American art。之後提到了她的繪圖特色，最後很明顯的使用貢獻 (contributions) 來提醒聽者注意。

2 **The Rainbow parrot is a species of <u>Australasian parrot</u>. It is a <u>medium-sized</u> bird, with a length ranging from <u>25–30cm</u> in size and a wingspan of about 17cm. The weight varies from <u>75–157g</u>.** (改寫自 http://en.wikipedia.org/wiki/Rainbow_Lorikeet)

情境篇

（彩虹鸚鵡是一澳洲的鸚鵡品種。它是一個中型的鳥類，身長 25-30 公分，羽翼約長 17 公分。體重從 75 到 157 公克各有不同。）

☑ species（*n.*）物種　☑ parrot（*n.*）鸚鵡

....

物品的描述重點在形容該物件的大小及功能，所以對數字的敏感度是必須的。在這個例子中物品是一種澳洲鸚鵡，在第一句就會直接說明物件的名稱。再者便是它的大小重量及相關可測量的數值。

3 **The young man in the shorts and sleeveless T-shirt stands in his boat and pulls it upstream with a long bamboo pole. The Onive River is shallow and moves swiftly against him. Overhead a brooding sky opens up and dispenses barrages of rain, then sunlight, then more rain.** （摘錄自 http://ngm.nationalgeographic.com/print/2010/09/madagascar/draper-text）

（這穿著短褲、無袖汗衫的年輕男子站在小船上用長竹竿向上游划。Onive 河水流淺而急地朝他流著。頭頂上大片的天空展開並下起雨，時而有陽光又時而有雨。）

☑ upstream（*adj.*）向上流的、逆流的

....

在描述景色時，說話者會利用語言使聽者在腦中建構畫面。

這個例子中想要描述河流上泛舟的船夫、以及背景陽光與水交替的光景。

景色描述由小的近的船夫 the young man 身上開始，再放大到描述河流 the Onive River 淺而急，再放更寬更遠到天空上 overhead a brooding sky 形容天氣的陰晴光影變化。

Part 3. ▸ **練習題** 【詳解請見 p213】

先聽一遍，找出描述的主題是人、物、或景。再依不同的主題多聽幾次，寫下重點。剛開始聽時可能只能聽到少數的資訊，試著寫下一些 key words，只要多聽幾次，對照單字解釋，再多聽多唸。切記不用心急，內容的理解沒有標準答案，多聽就能多了解。

① 🔊 MP3 **049**

提示字：Duncan, mother of modern dance

✎ 其他 key words：

② 🔊 MP3 **050**

提示字：the northern lights, arcs, clouds, streaks, green, purple, red

✎ 其他 key words：

③ 🔊 MP3 **051**

提示字：timepiece, dial, strap, water resistant, international warranty

✎ 其他 key words：

④ 🔊 MP3 **052**

提示字：boot jeans, light blue wash

✎ 其他 key words：

⑤ 🔊 MP3 **053**

提示字：sofa beds, 35 × 79

✎ 其他 key words：

6 🔊 MP3 **054**

提示字：Pablo Picasso, revolutionary artistic accomplishments

✍ 其他 key words：

7 🔊 MP3 **055**

提示字：Philadelphia, 2010 U.S. Census, Delaware Valley

✍ 其他 key words：

8 🔊 MP3 **056**

提示字：Harry Potter, Witchcraft, Wizardry, Dark Lord Voldemort

✍ 其他 key words：

Lesson 10

敘述

# Part 1.

要訣：如何聆聽「敘述類型」的資訊

　　敘述指的是描述事件或講述故事的方式。新聞報導中或電視電影中都常出現敘述故事的情形。練習聆聽敘述類型可以從三個方向著手：

一、凡是敘述類型都可能會出現的資訊有：主角，通常是人，以及時間及地點。雖然這些資訊中的專有名詞可能比較難聽懂，但不用過度緊張，重要的名詞會重複出現。

二、有別於描述類型，敘述型態的文章會有許多動詞，故在此動詞是聆聽者最需要掌握的重點。

三、在故事的最後，大多會有這事件所含的啓發，能夠抓住最後的結尾啓發便能輕易了解故事的重心。

🎵 Part 2。綜合範例

1 **The Tuck family** has **discovered** a spring whose water brings eternal life. A man **learns** their secret and **threatens to sell** the water to the highest bidder. **Mrs. Tuck kills the man** and is **jailed** and **sentenced** to be **executed**. Though the family **knows** she cannot be killed, they **worry** that their **secret** will be **revealed** when they try to kill her. (93 年學測)

（Tuck 家族發現一個可以使人永恆不死的泉水。有個男人知道了他們的秘密並威脅將泉水賣給高價收購者。Tuck 太太殺了這個男人，並且因此被關進牢且被判處行刑。雖然 Tuck 家人知道她不可能會被殺死但他們擔心當人們試圖殺她時，秘密將會被揭發。）

⊘ eternal（*adj.*）永恆的　⊘ bidder（*n.*）投標、投標人　⊘ sentence（*v.*）宣判
⊘ execute（*v.*）實施、處死

敘述故事時，人物時地等眾多資訊都會出現，但最重要的資訊就會不斷重複出現，如這個例子中的 Tuck 家族，以及 secret 都說出不只一次。另外，捉住動詞也可以幫助了解整個故事的發展；如 discover、learn、threaten to sell、kill、jailed、sentenced、executed、know、worry、reveal。若再加上對動詞的主詞受詞都有聽懂的話，其他小細節如果沒有聽清楚也可以猜得出來。

2 **On my second day in the mountains**, I **woke up** along with the sun to the pleasant fresh mountain air, **put on** my adventure shoes, and **prepared** for a day of **hiking**. Since I

was in no shape to tackle Snow Mountain, Taiwan's second-tallest mountain, I had to look for a trail more suitable for less-experienced hikers.（改寫自 http://www.go2taiwan.net/monthly_ selection.php?sqno=53）

（在山中的第二天，我隨著陽光以及山間清新空氣中醒來，穿上我的探險鞋以準備一整天的登山行程。既然我完全無法挑戰台灣的第二高峰雪山，我必須尋找一個較適合經驗少的登山者步道。）

在這個例子中第一句就說出了主角、時間及地點：I、my third day、in the mountains。之後隨著動詞及其他簡單可聽懂的單字更可以清楚的勾勒出事件的細節，如 woke up、sun、put on、prepared、hiking、tackle、look for a trail。另外、當聽到不熟悉的專有名詞時，千萬不用慌張，一則它可能會有同位語來進一步解說，如這裡的 Snow Mountain 就是 Taiwan's second-tallest mountain，再則它可能在接下來的談話中提到，所以如果聽不懂，也可以暫時忽略。

3 **The novel begins in the Shire, as Frodo inherits the Ring from Bilbo. Gandalf, a wizard, learns of the Ring's history and advises Frodo to take it away from the Shire. Frodo leaves, taking his friend, Sam, and two cousins, Merry and Pippin, as companions.**（改寫自 http://www.go2taiwan.net/monthly_ selection.php?sqno=53）

（小說開始於 Shire 村，當 Frodo 從 Bilbo 那繼承了戒指。Gandalf 巫師知道那戒指的來由並建議 Frodo 帶著它離開 Shire。Frodo 帶著他的朋友 Sam 以及表兄弟 Merry 和 Pippin 一同作伴離開。）

☑inherit（v.）繼承　☑companion（n.）同伴

這段「魔戒」的簡介是非常標準的敘述類型，背景地點清楚，人物按照時間順序一一出現，動詞也很多，讓人可以清楚想像故事的發展。重要的人名會一再出現，剛開始時也會有同位語顯示他的相關資料。The Ring 雖不是人，但也重複出現以顯示它的重要性。

◎ MP3 058

4 **To <u>Sherlock Holmes</u> she is always the woman. I have seldom <u>heard</u> him <u>mention</u> her under any other name. In his eyes she <u>eclipses and predominates</u> the whole of her sex. It was not that he <u>felt any emotion akin to love</u> for <u>Irene Adler</u>. All emotions, and that one particularly, were <u>abhorrent to his cold, precise but admirably balanced mind</u>.** （福爾摩斯短篇故事 A Scandal in Bohemia 波希米亞醜聞）

（對 Sherlock Holmes 而言，她一直是那個「女人」。我很少聽到他提到女人而不是指她。在他眼裡她遮蓋又主導了這個性別。不是說他對 Irene Adler 有類似愛的感情，因為所有情緒感覺，尤其是愛，都違背了他那冷酷、精準又令人欽羨的平衡心智。）

☑ eclipse（*n.*）蝕　☑ predominate（*v.*）佔主導地位
☑ abhorrent（*adj.*）令人憎惡的　☑ admirably（*adv.*）可令人讚美地

情境篇

人名、動作，都用了很多來敘述 Sherlock Holmes 對 Irene Adler 的特別。但因為也有對 Holmes 人物個性的敘述，就會有許多形容詞，如最後一句。這部分就比較像第一單元描述人物的用法了。

5 **<u>My wife</u> was <u>fascinated by the elegant calligraphy on the hand-written menu in a Chinese restaurant</u>. She <u>took it home</u> and <u>spent months</u> <u>knitting a sweater</u> with Chinese characters down the front. She was <u>wearing it</u> at a cocktail party when <u>a Chinese physician</u> <u>asked where she got the</u>**

symbols. "From a menu," she admitted. "<u>Do you know what they say</u>?" "I'm <u>afraid to ask</u>," my wife said, "but <u>tell me anyway</u>." "<u>Cheap, but good.</u>" （摘錄自 http://jokstop.com/0eg）

（我妻子為中國餐館手寫菜單上的優雅書法字著迷。她帶它回家並花了好幾個月將中文字織在毛衣胸前上，並穿去參加一個雞尾酒會。有個中國醫師問她是在哪裡找到這些字，她承認說「在餐單上。」「那麼妳知道它們代表什麼意思嗎？」我妻子說「我不敢問，但無論如何請你告訴我。」「價格便宜但好吃。」

☑fascinated（*adj.*）著迷的　☑calligraphy（*n.*）書法　☑knit（*v.*）編織
☑character（*n.*）漢字　☑physician（*n.*）醫生

....

這類型的小故事或笑話人物不多，動作或談話比較多。將人物、背景、以及所做出的事都劃線的話，不難發現幾乎每個字都是重點。但這類型的小故事用字不會太難聽懂，多聽幾次即可。另外小故事或笑話的重點都會是在最後一句突顯出來。

Part 3。 練習題 【詳解請見 p215】

根據上述說明,可以先將人物或主詞、地點、時間等資訊先試圖找出來,再者注意動詞的運用,最後再聽最後一句看看是否有任何重要訊息。千萬不要被聽不懂的字嚇到,多聽並分段來找出重點,再拼湊出整段含意。

① ◀》MP3 **059**

提示字:cautiously, wooden platform, fireflies

✍ 其他 key words:

② ◀》MP3 **060**

提示字:gun, Bob Green, gunshots

✍ 其他 key words:

③ ◀》MP3 **061**

提示字:alcohol, routine

✍ 其他 key words:

④ ◀》MP3 **062**

提示字:similarities, resume, profile, initial letter

✍ 其他 key words:

⑤ ◀》MP3 **063**

提示字:Christine, Angel of Music, deathbed

✍ 其他 key words:

情境篇

6 🔊 MP3 **064**

提示字：operator

✎ 其他 key words：

7 🔊 MP3 **065**

提示字：predict, forecast, leeches, moon, crickets

✎ 其他 key words：

8 🔊 MP3 **066**

提示字：pricks, Snow White

✎ 其他 key words：

9 🔊 MP3 **067**

提示字：railroad, occasions

✎ 其他 key words：

10 🔊 MP3 **068**

提示字：Amy, bumped, pausing, whopper

✎ 其他 key words：

Lesson 11

廣告

# Part 1.
要訣：先區分廣告的兩大類型

　　和一般口語或文章的英文句型不同，廣告中的英文句子都很簡短，沒有複雜的文法，或根本不需文法就能理解。除此之外，廣告中的用字重視修飾語，所以需要特別注意三種字詞的運用，包括名詞、動詞、形容詞或副詞。要學習聽懂廣告，可以先將其分為兩類來分析：

一、重點式：先點出品牌物件，多用動詞或名詞。
二、鋪陳式：先描寫印象，多用形容詞。

Point 1　重點式

◎ MP3 069

　　這類型的廣告會先講出品牌、關鍵字、或標語，再用簡明的字來描述產品特色。 通常動詞的運用在這種類型的廣告是比較著重的部分。

1 Elvin. Fewer pills. All-day relief. If you could take fewer pills, why wouldn't you? Just two Elvin have the strength to last all day.
（Elvin。少一點藥丸，一整天的輕鬆。如果你能服用少些藥丸，那為何不做呢？只要兩顆 Elvin，就能持續一整天的活力。）
☑ pill（n.）藥丸　☑ relief（n.）緩和、減輕痛苦

- -

一開始便點明產品名稱跟特色，接著，除了重複使用形容詞 fewer 以強調產品的優點之外，還使用明確的動詞 take、have 和 last 來加強聽者

的注意力，而且這些動詞後所接的受詞 fewer pills（更少的藥丸）、the strength（力量）和 all day（整天）更具有洗腦的功能，說服聽者採取行動。

2 I feed her Umaka. Bring out your breed's full potential. Get the most out of your dog with Umaka's five breed-specific formulas. Look for them at your local pet speciality store.

（我餵她 Umaka。激發你的寵物所有的潛能。藉由 Umaka 五種寵物特殊配方，可以從你的狗得到最多。請去當地的寵物店搜尋這些配方。）

☑ potential（*adj.*）潛在的　☑ formula（*n.*）慣例、配方
☑ speciality（*n.*）專長、特色

點出產品名稱後，清楚的動詞 bring out（帶出）、get（得到）加上正面的形容 full（滿的）、most（最多的），能明確的給予聽者指示，促使聽者跟著廣告中的建議去做，去 look for（尋找）。

3 BP College. Offering a new series of intensive classes designed to help you prepare for all kinds of college entrance tests. Be perfect. Come to BP College. Call 605-700-7997 now, or register at our website, www. BPcollege.com.

（BP 學院，提供一系列全新設計的密集課程，幫助你準備各式的入學考試。邁向完美，來 BP 學院。現在，請打 605-700-7997，或是在我們網站 www. BPcollege.com 上註冊。）

☑ entrance test（*n.*）入學考　☑ register（*v.*）註冊

一開始就表明產品或公司名稱，說出名號以後再解說商品內容，並且多使用動詞（offering、help you prepare、be、come、call、register）來促使聽者消費。

情境篇

◎ **MP3 070**

相反於上者，鋪陳式的廣告會將品牌或其關鍵標語在最後說出，之前會用許多形容來幫助鋪陳建構產品形象，所以在這類型的廣告中形容詞或用以形容的名詞比較重要。

1 Don't let its sleek, aerodynamic exterior fool you. Inside there's a world of smart, cargo-friendly design. It's the perfect combination of style, amenities and space. Introducing the all-new Accord Crosstour from Honda. （摘錄自 Crosstour Honda 電視廣告）

（不要讓它光滑又具流線型的外表欺騙你。他的內在設計是能方便載貨的智慧空間。它是品味、舒適與空間的完美結合。介紹您 Honda 全新 Accord Crosstour。）

☑ sleek（*adj.*）光滑的　☑ aerodynamic（*adj.*）空氣動力學的

☑ exterior（*n.*）外部　☑ cargo（*n.*）貨物

這個介紹車子的廣告中，運用了許多形容詞來描述車子的各個部分，如用 sleek、aerodynamic 來形容車子的外在；車子的內在則是 smart、cargo-friendly；兩者的結合是 perfect！最後提出品牌名稱，而且再用一個簡潔有力的形容詞 all-new 以強調這個新產品來提高消費者的購買慾。

2 Do they charge you if you use the card? Do they charge you if you don't use the card? Enough. No annual fee. No reward redemption fee. No inactivity fee. No additional card fee. Switch to the KSB More card today.

（他們在您用卡時跟您收費嗎？他們在您沒有用卡時跟您收費嗎？夠了！不用年費。不收退卡費。不收呆卡費。附卡也不收費。今天，換成 KSB

More 卡吧！）

☑ reward（*n.*）報酬　☑ redemption（*n.*）贖回　☑ inactivity（*n.*）靜止
☑ additional（*adj.*）額外的

一開始不講明產品，先用句型相同的問句讓觀眾聯想到自身使用信用卡的經驗，再使用連續四個疊字強調 No... fee，來描述並給予觀眾一種良好的情境：No annual fee. No reward redemption fee. No inactivity fee. No additional card fee.。雖然形容各種費用不一定是用形容詞，也很多是專有名詞，但整體而言是要描述這張信用卡不多收費用，給人很輕鬆的感覺。

3 We provide speed and reliability but with a minimal carbon footprint. We don't just deliver excellence, but a better future as well. Excellence. Simply delivered. DHL.

（摘錄自 www.dhl-brandworld.com/fashion）

（我們提供速度與可靠性，與最小的碳用量。我們不只運送優秀傑出，也創造更好的未來。卓越、絕對送達，DHL 快遞。）

☑ reliability（*n.*）可靠　☑ minimal（*adj.*）最小的
☑ carbon footprint（*n.*）碳耗用量

公司名稱最後才說出，而之前先用許多正面的形象形容商品，藉以給聽者洗腦。這個例子雖然不是用形容詞形容，而是用描述性與修飾性的名詞，但也有一樣效果，如 speed、reliability、a minimal carbon footprint、excellence、better future。最後甚至再用一句標語總結，再加上公司名稱以加強印象：Excellence. Simply delivered. DHL.

Part 2 ▸ 練習題 【詳解請見 p217】

請試著按照前面的分類來注意動詞和形容詞的運用。
剛開始聽時可能只能聽到少數的資訊，可參考每一題所列出的提示字，多聽幾遍，並試著寫出其他的 **key words**。

① 🔊 MP3 **071**

提示字：get, find, watch

✎ 其他 key words：

② 🔊 MP3 **072**

提示字：fossil fuel, helping to deliver, energy

✎ 其他 key words：

③ 🔊 MP3 **073**

提示字：sneezing, watery eyes, capsule, medicine, allergy

✎ 其他 key words：

④ 🔊 MP3 **074**

提示字：a used car, sedans, minivans

✎ 其他 key words：

⑤ 🔊 MP3 **075**

提示字：achieve, dreams, perfect home, Real Estate

✎ 其他 key words：

6 🔊 MP3 **076**

提示字：Mac, upgrade, a better computer

✍ 其他 key words：

7 🔊 MP3 **077**

提示字：multi- vitamin, adults 50, immunity, vitality, good health

✍ 其他 key words：

Lesson 12

氣象預報

🔑 Part 1。要訣：熟悉氣象基本用語

對初學者來說，氣象報告是練習聽力的最佳方式，因為氣象報告中通常只用名詞以及形容詞描述天氣，句子簡短也不會用太難的文法句型。故只要熟悉一些氣象的基本用語，不太需要文法的概念也能聽懂播報員說的話。

以下是氣象報告容易出現的重點字類型：

一、氣象類專有名詞
二、描寫天氣形容詞
三、方向位置
四、數字

Point 1 氣象類專有名詞

氣象報告中的專有名詞很多，包括氣象學的名稱以及地理位置的名稱，或是一些因天氣引起的現象等等，我們可能不熟悉，一般只要認識我們所居住地的相關情形就足夠，以下列了一些可能會常遇到的字：

- 颱風 typhoon
- 颶風 hurricane
- 龍捲風 tornado
- 風暴 storm
- 暴風雪 blizzard
- 霧 fog / mist

- 溫度 temperature（度 degree）
- 鋒面 front
- 低氣壓 low pressure
- 高氣壓 high pressure
- 寒流 / 熱浪 cold wave/ heat wave
- 紫外線 Ultraviolet

- 霜 **frost**
- 雲 **clouds**
- 雪 **snow**
- 雷雨 **thunderstorm**
- 陣雨 **shower**
- 路面濕滑 **slippery roads**
- 冰雹 **hail**

- 熱帶 **tropical zone**
- 副熱帶 **sub-tropical zone**
- 溫帶 **temperate zone**
- 淹水 **flood**
- 土石流 **mudslide / landslide**
- 停電 **blackout / power outage**

Point 2　描寫天氣形容詞

除了溫度和天氣概況，播報員也會用一些客觀或主觀的形容詞來描述天氣，如主觀的有：熱 hot、溫暖 warm、冷 cold、涼 cool、凍 freezing、寒 chilly 及客觀的有：乾燥 dry、潮濕 wet、有風 windy、有雨 rainy、有陽光 sunny、有雲 cloudy。

Point 3　方向位置

聆聽氣象時必須要先熟悉方位的用字，因為天氣解說時常使用八種方位來描述天氣走向以及地理位置：東 east、南 south、西 west、北 north，以及東南 southeast、東北 northeast、西南 southwest、西北 northwest。例如，東北季風 northeast front 或北大西洋 North Atlantic。

注意，中文是以東西來定位，如說東南、東北、西南、西北，都是以「東」或「西」開始；英文則以「南」或「北」定位，所以是 southeast、southwest、northeast、northwest。

　　氣象預報中，一定會出現數字來表示日期以及溫度。溫度又分為攝氏 centigrade 或 Celsius（℃）跟華氏 Fahrenheit（℉）。在聽預報之前必須先對背景以及即將聽到的數字範圍有心理準備，聽到的時候就能馬上抓住資訊。例如一般春天大約在 10-25℃或 70-90℉左右。

ⓐ Part 2。 綜合範例

1 **On the 16th, a cold front will bring heavy rain and possible thunderstorms. From the 19th to the 22nd, there will be few showers but some areas in the north may experience heavy fog.**

（16 號，一道冷鋒將帶來大雨並可能有雷陣雨。19 到 22 號將會有些小雨，但部分北部地區會有大霧。）

把握住前面所提的幾個重點字，整段氣象預報的內容就不難了解了。重點都在名詞等相關的氣象用法。

2 **The forecast tonight is for further rain, heavy in parts of the north and west UK, becoming drier by dawn. The temperature overnight may drop as low as five degrees below zero.**

（今天晚上的天氣有更多的雨，英國北部及西部地區部分有大雨，到清晨會變乾燥一些。夜間氣溫會降到攝氏負 5 度。）

⊘ dawn（n.）黎明

氣象報告中的句子都不會太長，所以把握重點字就可以猜出意思。把握地點（north and west UK）、時間（tonight and overnight）、關於氣象的形容詞或名詞（rain 和 drier）、以及數字相關的資訊。

3 **A spokesperson from the Meteorological Research Bureau said that downpours flooded several small towns in**

southeastern Colorado last night and have already caused landslides. Residents along several rivers were warned to move out of their houses immediately.

（氣象調查局的發言人說，昨晚豪雨淹沒了 Colorado 東南部地區數個小鎮並且已經引發土石流，河邊的居民被警告要即時撤離家園。）

☑ Meteorological Research Bureau（n.）氣象調查局

☑ landslides（n.）土石流　☑ resident（n.）居民

跟氣象報告有關的也包括天氣引起的災難，如地震 earthquake、洪水 flood、停電 blackout、土石流 landslide 等等。比較嚴重的情形時會請教政府機關的專業氣象調查 Meteorological Research Bureau 來說明，並解釋必要的措施及警告。

4 **A heatwave in the United States smashed temperature records last weekend. It was caused by multiple high pressure systems. The high temperature in Dallas yesterday was 42 degrees and it was 43 in Newark. Unfortunately, the extremely hot weather will not end soon and is expected to continue for at least another week.**

（上周末美國熱浪打破了氣溫的記錄。這是多個高氣壓造成。昨天 Dallas 高溫 42 度而 Newark 有 43 度。很不幸地，這極度的高溫不會這麼快結束而且還可能會持續一個星期。）

☑ smash（v.）粉碎

氣象報告分為兩部分，一是分析已經發生的狀況，二是對未來天氣做預測。第一部分比較可能出現專有的氣象名詞，若是對專業分析沒有興趣或是聽不懂，後半段的預測通常都比較簡單，只著重於大略的溫度範圍跟天象。

Part 3 ▸ 練習題 【詳解請見 p220】

先熟悉上述的氣象類用字，仔細聽氣象預報並填入空格中的單字或數字。

1 🔊 MP3 **079**

The weather forecast for today and tomorrow in Taiwan is for _____s
and intermittent _____ up _____ and in the _____.
There will be _____ but no _____ in central and _____
Taiwan.

2 🔊 MP3 **080**

Ferilla is also _____ and _____. Its beautiful beaches are
closed because of the _____. People who had hoped to a vacation
there will have to change their plans. The city's temperature today is
_____ ˚C .

3 🔊 MP3 **081**

Today is a _____ day. After a whole week of _____
_____, the sun has finally reappeared. Now, let's look at the current
temperatures: _____ up _____; _____ Mid-island and in
the _____, and _____ down _____.

4 🔊 MP3 **082**

Today's weather will be _____ and _____ but _____ with
temperatures _____ below _____ by the end of the day.
_____ and _____ will be mostly _____ with partly
_____ weather in the _____ mountain areas. This _____,

southerly winds should push the high back up to near _____
degrees.

⑤ ◀》MP3 **083**

Now it is time for the weather report. After all the _____ we've
enjoyed, you might be disappointed to hear that a cold _____
will bring a _____ _____ _____ _____ tomorrow
with temperatures around _____ degrees Celsius. Overnight lows
tonight will be _____ _____, possibly reaching _____
in some areas. But don't worry. Conditions will clear up by _____
_____ with temperatures in the _____ _____ and clear
skies are forecast for the weekend.

⑥ ◀》MP3 **084**

The weather today will be as _____ as yesterday, but tomorrow
and the next day will be very _____. A _____ system will
move in from the south. We expect some gusts of up to _____
_____ per hour then. _____ have been issued for drivers and
road workers.

⑦ ◀》MP3 **085**

A _____ _____ _____ has been issued by the weather
bureau. A _____ _____ will bring _____ conditions to the
mountain areas of Southern California this _____. Residents should
prepare for _____ and travelers should postpone their plans.

Lesson 13
新聞英語

要訣：化解新聞英語的三大難題

新聞英語一直是大家覺得困難度最高的種類，其實困難是因為會有很多的專有名詞，在聽起來不熟悉的情狀下很容易就失去焦點。以下將分為三類分析，將困難點化解開並多聽多練習，新聞英文就不會很難聽懂了：

一、新字彙：① 衍生字 ② 複合字 ③ 縮頭字 ④ 縮寫字
二、結構：倒三角結構（標題、導言、本文、細節）
三、句法：常用句型與慣用語

Point 1 新字彙

新聞中常常會有新的用字出現，在聽不懂的狀態下就會失去信心。但這些字其實都是從舊的字中延伸出來的。我們可以分為四種延伸字：

1. 衍生字 由慣用字根 + 單字而成。

例如：**semiconductor**（semi 半 +conductor 導體）半導體、**ecosystem**（eco 生態 +system 系統）生態系統

2. 複合字 由兩個或以上的單字所構成。

例如：**oil-free**（油 + 無）無油、brainwash（腦 + 洗）洗腦、**under-the-table deal**（下面 + 桌子 + 交易）檯面下的交易

3. 縮頭字 機構等專有名稱的第一個字的大寫構成。

例如：**WTO**（World Trade Organization）世界貿易組織、**ECFA**（Economic Cooperation Framework Arrangement）經濟合作架構協議

4. 縮寫字 由一個較長的字縮短而成。

例如：**ad**（advertisement）廣告、**flu**（influenza）流行性感冒、**Xmas**（Christmas）聖誕節

Point 2 結構

　　新聞英文不論是何種類型，結構上幾乎千篇一律是倒三角形。最上面的事最重要，越往下越是細節。所以按照重要性排列，先是最開頭的標題，再來是導言，再來是本文跟細節，最後可能還會有一些相關的提問。

1. 標題：最重要。是整個事件的一句重點大綱。
2. 導言：含有事件的起始原因或相關背景資料。
3. 本文：詳細說明事件的始末。
4. 細節：其他的資料，如相關人事的話語引述。

Point 3 句法

　　新聞中使用的句型不外乎是將前面標題的重點句及基本資料再用其他語法更詳細的說明。

1. 常用句型

- **S + ... + V**：主詞後會接他的工作職位或相關資料補充說明，再接動詞
- **Ving（Ved, To-V）, S + V**：先寫分詞，再接主要句子
- **S + V, Ving（Ved）**：先寫主要句子，再接分詞
- **With + N +（Ving, Ved）, S + V**：先用 with（隨著）某人或事的狀態，再接句子
- **Phrase, S + V**：開頭用片語表示狀況
- **" ... " said Sb; Sb said, "..."**：引述某人的說詞
- **S + V + that S + V**：用 that 連接兩個句子
- **Adv Clause, S + V**：副詞子句表示資料，再接主要句子
- **S, Adj clause, V**：用形容詞子句形容主詞，再接動作

2. 慣用語

- **according to reliable sources ...** 根據可靠消息……
- **decline to comment on the speculation ...** 拒絕對猜測做評論……
- **on the basis of ...** 基於……
- **refuse to comment on the report ...** 拒絕對報導做評論……
- **reach consensus on several issues ...** 達到共識……
- **quoted unidentified sources as saying ...**
  引用身分不明的來源指出……
- **speaking on condition of anonymity ...** 匿名者指出……

◎ Part2。綜合範例

1 Car Bombs Strike Second Major Iraq Bank

BAGHDAD—**A pair of car bombs detonated outside Iraq's Bank of Trade on Sunday morning, killing 26 people and wounding 52.**

There were no claims of responsibility for the bombing, but the Islamic State of Iraq has said it was responsible for a bloody raid at Iraq's Central Bank in Baghdad last Sunday that killed 15 people and injured 50.

"They try to harm the economic situation because they want to keep international companies from investing here," said Dr. Jabir al-Jabiri, a newly elected member of Parliament. （改寫自 The New York Times June 21, 2010.）

分析這篇新聞報導中的結構如下：

【標題：重點事件】汽車炸彈攻擊伊拉克第二主要銀行

【導言：相關背景資料】巴格達——一對汽車炸彈星期天早上在伊拉克貿易銀行外引爆，有 26 人死亡 52 人受傷。

【本文：詳述事件細節】對炸彈事件沒有任何聲明，但伊拉克的伊斯蘭部說它應該為上星期天巴格達中央銀行的血腥襲擊負責，該行動造成 15 人死亡 50 人受傷。

【細節：其他細節如引述某些人的評論】新上任的國會議員 Jabir al-Jabiri 博士說：「他們試圖傷害經濟情況因為他們想要阻止國際企業在這裡投資。」

⊘detonate（v.）爆炸、觸發　⊘wound（v.）使……受傷

✓bloody raid（n.）血腥攻擊　✓parliament（n.）議會、國會

◎ MP3 087

2 BP Chief Draws Outrage for Attending Yacht Race

BP's chief executive, <u>Tony Hayward</u>, spent the day off the coast of England watching his yacht compete in one of the world's largest races.

Two days after Mr. Hayward angered lawmakers on Capitol Hill with his refusal to provide details during testimony about the worst offshore <u>oil spill</u> in United States history.

"He is having some rare private time with his son," a BP spokeswoman, Sheila Williams, said in a telephone interview on Saturday.（改寫自 The New York Times June 20, 2010.）

分析這篇新聞報導中的結構如下：

【標題：重點事件】BP 公司的執行長引起憤怒因其參與快艇賽

【導言：相關背景資料】BP 公司的執行長 Tony Hayward 休假一天去觀看他的快艇比賽，在英國海岸邊世界最大的快艇比賽之一。

【本文：詳述事件細節】兩天後，他引發美國國會立法委員的大怒，因為他拒絕在證詞中提供關於美國歷史上近海最糟漏油事件的詳細資料。

【細節：其他細節如引述某些人的評論】BP 公司的發言人 Sheila Williams 在一個星期六的電話訪問中說：「他正與他的兒子度過難得的私人時間。」

✓outrage（n.）暴怒　✓yacht（n.）遊艇　✓chief executive（n.）最高首長
✓testimony（n.）證詞　✓offshore（adj.）近海的

◎ MP3 088

3 The Roadway Was Shut Down for Fear of the Explosion

A five-car collision on Tennyson Avenue caused heavy traffic this afternoon during rush hour. Nobody was injured, but the roadway was shut down when one of the cars caught fire. There was fear of possible explosion. Investigators said that the accident was likely caused by a drunk driver.

【標題：重點事件】惟恐爆炸而封閉道路

【導言：相關背景資料】在今天下午交通顛峰時刻，一起五輛車的連環車禍造成了 Tennyson 街嚴重的塞車。

【本文：詳述事件細節】沒有人受傷，但道路因為有一台車著火了而封閉，怕是會造成爆炸。

【細節：其他細節如引述某些人的評論】調查員說這件意外很可能是因為酒駕而引起。

短篇的新聞不一定會有完整豐富的資料，尤其是像現場即時報導，即使還來不及做出仔細的調查，新聞仍會短篇幅的報導，但結構仍然一樣。最重要的是要聽出新聞主要發表的事件為何，以及相關地點時間等等資訊，其實也就是像上一章最後一結所要強調的重要資訊的掌握，記得抓住 5W1H 的原則以掌握重點，如劃線的部分。這篇的重點就在於道路封閉的原因與確切的時間地點。

- collision（*n.*）碰撞　- investigator（*n.*）調查員

◎ MP3 089

4 **In today's economic news, The Dow Jones Industrial Average rose sharply after Congress approved a $5 billion loan to the ailing banking sector. Banking stocks were up over 10%, and high-technology stocks also appeared to benefit from the bailout. They were up 5%. Most critics**

remain pessimistic about the long term prospects for the market and believe that it won't recover until 2013.

【標題：重點事件】今天的經濟新聞，道瓊工業指數大幅上漲

【導言：相關背景資料】因為議會通過以 50 億元的貸款資助疲弱的銀行業。

【本文：詳述事件細節】銀行股上漲 10%，而高科技股也受惠於這個資助方案，上漲 5%。

【細節：其他細節如引述某些人的評論】但大部分的評論家仍對長期市場保持悲觀的態度，他們相信直到 2013 年情形才會恢復正常。

新聞報導不會拐彎抹角的表達事件，而且是以一種很客觀公正的說法敘述事件。聽的人才會因為關心的要點不同而可能有不同的重點。劃線的部分包含各種可能的重點，但若是關心法案的人會注意的，就一定不會和注意股票趨勢的人相同。短線操作的人也會和注意長期發展的人的重點不同。

⊘congress（*n.*）代表大會　⊘ailing（*adj.*）生病的、體衰的

⊘bailout（*n.*）緊急財務援助

情境篇

Part 3 ▶ 練習題 【詳解請見 p220】

以下練習題為各類型新聞的部分或大綱，仔細聽並記下重點訊息，盡可能找出多些資訊，最後並試著找出文章的倒三角架構。

① 🔊 MP3 **090**

提示字：suspect, combat, colonization, Muslims

✍ 其他 key words：

② 🔊 MP3 **091**

提示字：bullet train, struck from behind, killing, injuring, power outage

✍ 其他 key words：

③ 🔊 MP3 **092**

提示字：famous tennis player, she is back, defeat, consistent

✍ 其他 key words：

④ 🔊 MP3 **093**

提示字：passed, federal law, health insurance, financial burden

✍ 其他 key words：

⑤ 🔊 MP3 **094**

提示字：hired, be acted, in talks to, casting

✍ 其他 key words：

Lesson 14

休閒娛樂

🔑 Part 1.
要訣：具備情境單字和內容字

在國外的休閒娛樂不外乎是跟朋友聚餐或是出外參加活動表演，一般也是一些日常生活用語。以下列出這些休閒場所，雖然不盡相同，但只要把握住情境單字以及內容字，就不難聽懂。也就是說，還是必須具備相關情境單字的知識，以及掌握以動詞、名詞為主的內容字。

一、餐廳點餐
二、觀看比賽或表演
三、購物：商場廣播以及須付帳的方式（cash、check or credit card）

Point 1　餐廳點餐

餐廳點餐可以分為在餐廳用餐或是外帶，通常速食店比較容易會外帶，而且對話也比較簡單。在餐廳用餐會有點餐或聆聽服務生說明菜單的內容的情形。

◎ MP3 **095**

1 在餐廳

A: May I have the menu, please? I would like to order now. What is the specialty of the house?

B: Our goose fillet steak is the most delicious in town.

A: Ok, I want one.

B: How do you like your steak?

A: Well done, please.

（A：請給我菜單好嗎？我想要點菜。

你們店裡的招牌是什麼？

B：我們的鵝肝醬菲力牛排是全鎮最好吃的。

A：好，我要一份。

B：你的牛排要幾分熟？

A：麻煩全熟。）

....

第一二句的詢問菜單跟點菜是慣用句。點菜一般會有圖片，所以不知道所有菜色名稱也沒關係。

◎ MP3 096

2 在速食店

A: I want two number 3 meals, both with coke, a couple of French fries, and a bucket of fried chicken. To go, thanks. And could you please put extra napkins inside?

B: Of course. Your order will be ready in just a few minutes.

（A：我要兩個三號餐，都附可樂，一份薯條，還有一桶炸雞。帶走，謝謝。可以請你多放一些紙巾進去嗎？ B：當然。您的餐點幾分鐘內就會準備好。）

☑ to go 外帶　☑ napkin（*n.*）餐巾

Point 2 觀看比賽或表演

◎ MP3 097

在國外看運動比賽是很常見的休閒活動。競賽中會播報進行的狀態跟戰況，其中字句都不會很長，但聆聽前必須先對該項運動的專有字詞有一定程度的了解才好聽懂。以美式足球為例：

1 Here comes San Diego's running back, Robinson! He fakes everyone out! He runs so fast that no one can catch him! Here comes Robinson! He gets to the end zone, 98-yard touchdown!

（San Diego 的跑鋒 Robinson 來了！他騙過所有人！他跑太快了！沒有人追得過他！他來了！得分！98 碼的達陣！）

✓touchdown（*n.*）達陣（美式足球）　✓fake（*v.*）騙過

聽不懂專用術語就很難了解，反之了解術語就能很容易聽懂，因為現場轉播都不會用太難的句子。Running back 跑鋒、touchdown 達陣。

觀看表演的項目有很多，例如看電影、聽音樂會、看各種秀等等。不論何種表演節目，都有可能聽到類似的廣播或公告，所以只要注意內容字就可以得到重要的訊息。

2 The doors will be kept closed except between acts. Please turn off your cellphones. Photography, videotaping and audiotaping are strictly prohibited. The show will begin in 10 minutes.

（除了換幕之外，大門將會關閉。請關掉你的手機。嚴禁攝影、錄影、及錄音。表演將在 10 分鐘後開始。）

✓photography（*n.*）攝影　✓videotape（*v.*）錄影　✓audiotape（*v.*）錄音
✓strictly（*adv.*）嚴格地　✓prohibit（*v.*）禁止

這是一般表演場地都會有的廣播內容。注意內容字就可以知道主要傳達的意思。

去看電影其實不會遇到太多需要交談的情形，只要說明清楚片名跟時間就能買票，現在甚至很多電影票都是在網路上就可以訂購的。關於電影的對話比較常發生在朋友之間的對談。

A: What would you like to see this afternoon?

B: Has Brad Pitt's new film been released yet?

A: No, it will be released this weekend, so we have to wait for two days. But this week, there is another action movie by Colin Farrell. I heard that it is great.

B: But I want to see a comedy. I am exhausted and need a laught.

A: OK, I know what we should see—Jim Carrey's "Mr. Popper's Penguins."

B: Sounds great!

A：你今天下午想看什麼？

B：Brad Pitt 的新片上映了嗎？

A：沒有，這個周末才會上映，所以我們還要再等兩天。但這禮拜，有另一部 Colin Farrell 的動作片，我聽說很棒。

B：但我想看喜劇。我筋疲力盡，需要笑一下。

A：好！我知道我們應該看什麼了，Jim Carrey 的 "波普先生的企鵝"。

B：聽起來很棒。

在此列出各種類型的電影，對於訂購電影票或與人聊電影都很有幫助。

喜劇電影 comedy film

商業電影 commercial film

實驗電影 experimental film

記錄片 documentary film

愛情文藝片 romance film

動作片 action film

驚悚片 thriller film

恐怖片 horror film

災難片 disaster film

動畫片 animated feature

劇情片 feature film

奇幻電影 fantasy film

懸疑片 mystery & suspense film

黑幫電影 gangster film

預告片 trailer

情境篇

◎ MP3 098

　　出國旅遊購買物品時最需要注意的英文聽力在於購物廣場的廣播、付帳時的方式、以及事後退換貨的對談。對於數字的用法雖然也不同，但可以用阿拉伯數字顯示。在國外付帳的方式分為三種：現金、支票、以及信用卡。另外也要注意最後帳單上會另加 10%~15% 稅金等我國沒有的習慣。

1 Welcome to SQ Mall. We are open <u>weekdays</u> from <u>10 a.m. to 7 p.m.</u> On <u>weekends</u>, the mall closes <u>at 5 p.m.</u> If you would like a <u>map</u> of the mall, please stop by <u>the information booth</u>, which is located at <u>the entrance</u> to <u>the food court</u>. Thank you.

（歡迎來到 SQ 百貨，我們平日營業時間是從早上 10 點到晚上 7 點，周末於下午五點打烊。如果你需要本店的地圖，請到位於食品陳列區入口處的服務台領取，謝謝。）

....

購物商場可能隨時會廣播訊息，在不清楚自己想要知道何種訊息時，要注意數字、時間、地點等名詞。

2 A: I'll take this coat and these two pairs of pants.

　 B: Yes, please wait for a moment. That comes to <u>$50.45</u>. Are you paying by <u>cash, check, or credit card</u>?

　 A: Cash. Here you are.

　 B: Thank you. Here is your change. Have a nice day. Bye.

（A：我要這件外套跟這兩件褲子。

　B：好的，請稍候。總共 50 元 45 分。你要付現金、支票、還是刷信用卡？

　A：現金。在這裡。）

B：謝謝你。零錢找你。祝你今天愉快，再見。

....

錢幣的說法在元 dollar 後面的分會有不同的用法，如一分是 cent、十分是 dime、25 分是 quarter。一般商店會有收據可以看清楚，市場的攤販就必須要聽清楚了。

【詳解請見 p222】

請聆聽以下對話或廣播，並寫出可能的發生地點。

① 🔊 MP3 **099**

提示字：Lions, Bears, two seconds, win, a point

✎ 發生地點：

② 🔊 MP3 **100**

提示字：Tommy Ribs, menus, take your order

✎ 發生地點：

③ 🔊 MP3 **101**

提示字：suitcase, the handle, receipt, exchange, company policy

✎ 發生地點：

④ 🔊 MP3 **102**

提示字：return, exchanges, smaller size, any in stock

✎ 發生地點：

Lesson 15

旅行觀光

🔑 Part 1. 要訣：旅遊必備三類資訊

　　赴國外自助旅遊時，即使是不懂英文的情形下一般也能夠得到輔助資料，如旅遊地點的中文簡介或圖示，但是沿途中仍可能會聽到一些必須了解的資訊，尤其是特殊事件的廣播，以下列出幾種可能的情況：

一、搭乘交通工具：注意班次、時間、地點等資訊
二、飯店溝通：包括預訂房 reservation、入住 check in、退房 check out
三、參加旅遊行程導覽

Point 1　搭乘交通工具

◎ MP3 **103**

　　搭乘交通工具時雖然會有書面的搭乘資訊，但在途中仍有廣播訊息需要聆聽並理解，以免會有錯過班次或搭錯車的問題。在注意這類的廣播時，事先如能記下自己所要搭乘的班次、時間、以及地點等重要字彙，聽的時候就比較能理解。

1 Welcome to the Airport Express. This train will stop at Tsing Yi, Kowloon and Central Hong Kong. Next station, Tsing Yi. Passengers transfering to the Tung Chung Line and East Rail Line, please change trains at this station. Doors will open on the left. Please take your baggage with you.

（歡迎搭乘機場快線，本班車將會到達青衣、九龍以及香港市中心。下一站，青衣。 要轉乘東涌線及東鐵線的乘客，請在下一站下車。 門將於左

邊開啓，請攜帶你的行李。）

．．

搭乘交通工具要先知道自己所要搭乘的線路名稱與站名並小心聆聽，以免坐錯。

2 Attention please. This is an announcement for passengers on East Airline's flight ES475. The boarding gate has been changed to Gate 10, Gate 10. Passengers on ES475, please go to Gate 10 before 9:30 for boarding.

（請注意，這是東方航空班機 ES475 的廣播。ES475 班機的登機門改為 10 號門、10 號門。請搭乘 ES475 班機的乘客在 9:30 前去 10 號門登機。）

．．

除了清楚自己要搭乘的航班號碼，其他相關的數字如時間、地點也要特別注意。

Point 2 飯店溝通

◎ MP3 **104**

需要與飯店溝通的主要情形在於房間的預定、辦理入住或退房的相關應對。只要聽清楚櫃檯人員所說的日期時間及房數，應該就沒有大礙了。其他情形只要打電話到客房服務部 Room Service 一般都可以得到解決。

1 A: Howard Hotel. Good evening.

B: Could I make a reservation, please?

A: Yes, certainly. When would you like to make a reservation for?

B: I would like to make a reservation for a standard room for two people on May 19.

A: Our check in time is 2 p.m. and the check out time is 12 p.m. Is that Ok with you?

A：Howard 飯店晚安你好。

B：我想訂房。

A：沒問題，請問要訂哪天？

B：我想訂一間 2 個人的商務套房，5 月 19 號。

A：我們的客房入住時間是 2 點，退房房間是 12 點。這樣可以嗎？

2 A: Hi, this is Mr. Miller in room 1012. The pipe under the sink in my bathroom is leaking.

B: We'll send somebody right away.

A: It's not just dripping. A steady stream of water is coming out. I'm afraid that it will flood.

B: Yes, we'll come immediately. And we could move you to another room if the repairs bother you.

A: Let me think about that.

A：你好，我是 1012 號房的 Miller 先生。我浴室裡水槽下的水管在漏水。

B：我們馬上派人過來。

A：它不只是滴水而已。持續的有水流出，我很怕是要淹水了。

B：好的，我們立刻來。我們可以替您換到另一間房以防修理時會打擾到您。

A：我考慮一下。

☑leak（v.）漏水　☑stream（n.）小河、溪流

◎ MP3 **105**

　　若是參加旅行團會有領隊及會說中文的導遊，但自助旅行時也可能參加當地短暫的導覽，在沒有翻譯的情形下，仍是可以聽懂主要內容。一般會給予書面資料，先大致翻過就能有初步了解，其他內容會因為參觀物不同而異，重點就盡量記下就可以。一般導覽都會先簡介行程內容，注意時間上的安排以免脫隊。

1 Attention, ladies and gentlemen, our driver will stop here in Canterburry for <u>four</u> hours. You can find many <u>top-quality</u> <u>restaurants</u> around here, so this will be a great opportunity to try some local <u>delicacies</u>. I would also <u>recommend</u> that you take some time to visit the <u>historical sites</u> here in Canterburry. <u>On</u> <u>your left</u> is the <u>oldest building</u> in the city, <u>the Old Canterburry</u> <u>Church</u>, which is almost <u>500</u> years old. Another point of interest is the <u>Martial Museum</u>, where you will have the chance to view many kinds of local weaponry.

（各位先生小姐請注意，我們的司機會在 Canterburry 這裡停留四個小時。你可以在這附近找到許多頂級餐廳，這可是個嚐試當地美食的好機會。我也推薦你們花點時間去參觀這裡的一些歷史古蹟。在你的左邊是 Canterburry 最老的建築物，幾乎有 500 年歷史的 Canterburry 大教堂。另一個景點是軍事博物館，在那裡你有機會看到許多種當地武器。）

　✓ martial（*adj.*）戰爭的、軍事的　✓ weaponry（*n.*）軍備、武器

除了時間以外，一些重要景點的位置也值得多注意。

Part 2。 練習題 【詳解請見 p224】

聆聽下列旅遊中可能會遇到的廣播或對話，試著將重要的資訊填入劃線處。

🔈 MP3 **106**

Your attention please! Train No. _____ bound for _____ is now approaching the platform and will depart at _____. Please proceed with boarding immediately and mind the platform gap when you board the train. We wish you a pleasant journey!

🔈 MP3 **107**

A: Denver International Airport. Good morning.

B: I saw a news report about some _____ near Denver, and I'm worried about my flight _____. That means there will be changes to the flight schedule, right?

A: Yes, you're right. All flights are _____ due to poor visibility. We expect the fog to lift by noon tomorrow. About the new schedule, you can check our _____ before you leave. We update the schedule every _____ hours.

B: Ok, I'll check the website. Thank you.

A: No problem. Thank you for calling.

🔈 MP3 **108**

Good evening ladies and gentlemen, this is your captain speaking. In a few minutes we will be entering an area with strong _____. Please _____ to your seats, _____ your seatbelts, and remain seated until the fasten seatbelts light is _____ _____. Also please make sure that your bags are stowed properly in the _____ compartments or _____ the seat in front of you. If you need an air _____ _____, it can be found in the pouch in front of you. If you have any other questions or need anything, please contact our flight staff by pressing the _____ _____ _____ _____.

④ 🔊 MP3 **109**

Attention, please. We regret to inform you that _____ _____ _____ _____ scheduled to depart at _____ for _____ has been delayed due to the _____. All passengers scheduled to depart on that flight should stand by until further notice. If you have any questions about the delay or _____ flights, please contact the customer service desk located in front of Gate _____.

⑤ 🔊 MP3 **110**

A: Good afternoon. _____ _____?

B: Yes.

A: Do you have _____?

B: Yes. I do. My name is _____ _____.

A: Welcome! Let me see my list .... Here it is. Miss Wang, you need a _____ room for _____ days. Is that correct?

B: That is correct.

A: Would you please fill out this registration form. And please _____ here.

Lesson 16

電話溝通

🔑 Part 1. 要訣：掌握電話習慣用語

英文的電話溝通應該是最有可能出現在日常生活中的應用了。除了一些特殊習慣用語外，可能出現的情境種類並不多。以下列出一些習慣用語並指出三種常見的情境：

一、慣用語
二、一般情境：A. 詢問資訊 B. 抱怨 C. 預約

Point 1 慣用語

電話用語跟一般對話不同的地方有五個：

1. hello ...：「喂」
2. This is ...：「我是……」或「這裡是……」
3. would like ...：表示禮貌的「想要」
4. hold on：「等一下」
5. hang up：掛掉電話

情境篇

Point 2 一般情境

◎ MP3 **111**

請注意以下英文畫底線部分，為對話中的重要資訊。

包括找人、問時間或地點等等，也常會遇到需要留言或轉接的時候。

1 A: Good morning. Mr. Milton's office. How may I help you?

B: This is Bill Walton. I'd like to speak to Mr. Milton, please.

A: He's answering an international call at the moment. Would you like to hold or leave a message?

B: Okay, please tell him Smith and Wilson definitely will come, Campbell and Johnson won't, and no one knows what Stern will do. Mr. Milton will understand. That's all. Thanks.

（A：Milton 先生辦公室，你早！有什麼需要我效勞的嗎？

B：我是 Bill Walton。我找 Milton 先生。

A：他現在正在接一通國際電話，你要等一下還是留言？

B：好，那麻煩你告訴他 Smith 和 Wilson 絕對會來，Campbell 和 Johnson 不會，沒有人知道 Stern 會怎樣。Milton 先生會了解。就這樣，謝謝。）

☑hold（v.）等一下　☑leave a message 留言

詢問資訊類的電話在禮貌問候，記下一些必要的資訊，尤其是對方需要留言轉達的時候。

2 The number you've dialed, 353-8680, has been <u>changed</u> to 909-1012. If you wish to be <u>connected</u> to the new number, press the pound key. You will be <u>charged</u> $2 for the connection service.

（您打的這支電話 353-8680 已經改成 909-1012。如果您想要轉接到這支新的電話號碼，請按 # 字鍵。將會向您收取 2 元的轉接服務費。）

☑change（v.）改變　☑connect（v.）轉接　☑charge（v.）收費

語音電話裡的資訊通常不會說得太快，也可以重複聽。重要的是數字。

B. 抱怨

抱怨電話通常會比較冗長，但必須記下抱怨的原因以及處理的方法。

3 A: Hello, I'm Gin Lynn. I'm calling to see if the <u>sweaters I ordered last month have been sent out</u> yet. I've been <u>waiting for a long time</u>. Your people said I would get them in 10 days.

B: <u>Due to the typhoon</u>, the container ships couldn't leave for a week. I'm sorry to say that you won't get the shipment until next month.

A: Next month! Oh, no, what can I do?

B: Unfortunately, there's not a lot we can do for you except apologize for the delay.

（A：你好，我是 Gin Lynn。我打電話來問問我上個月訂的毛衣寄送了沒有。我等很久了。你們的人説我會在 10 天內拿到。

B：因爲颱風的關係，貨運船一個星期都不能來。很抱歉，直到下個月你都不會收到貨。

A：下個月！喔！不！那我該怎麼辦？

B：很不幸地，除了道歉我們能爲你做的也不多。）

C. 預約

電話預約使用機會很多，包括訂餐廳、機票、表演、看病等等。對話模式也都差不多，只要記好預約的時間、人數等資料。最後對方都會再重複一次來確認。

4 A: Seashore Restaurant. How may I help you?

B: I'd like to reserve a table for <u>tomorrow night at 7:30</u>, and I would like a table near the window.

A: For how many people, please? The largest table we have near the window is for eight.

B: Oh, we have six people.

A: A table for six people near the window at 7:30 tomorrow, right? May I take your name, sir?

B: Oh, of course. This is David Ford.

A: Mr. Ford, thank you for your reservation. See you tomorrow.

（A：海岸餐廳，有什麼可以效勞的嗎？

　B：我想要訂位，明天晚上 7:30，要靠窗的桌子。

　A：請問有幾位？靠窗最大的桌子是 8 個人。

　B：喔，我們有 6 位。

　A：一個六人的靠窗的桌子，明天晚上 7:30，對嗎？ 先生，可以給我您的姓名嗎？

　B：喔，當然。我是 David Ford。

　A：Ford 先生，謝謝您的訂位，明天見。）

5 A: This is Sandy Cooper. I'm calling to confirm my reservation for tonight.

B: I'm sorry, Miss Cooper, but I can't find any rooms reserved in your name.

A: That's impossible! I asked my secretary to book it last week.

B: Don't worry, Miss Cooper. We still have several vacant suites. I'll reserve one for you right now.

（A：我是 Sandy Cooper，我打來確認我今天晚上的預約。

　B：很抱歉，Cooper 小姐，我沒有看到任何訂房紀錄在您的名下。

　A：怎麼可能？我上星期叫我秘書訂的。

　B：別擔心，Cooper 小姐，我們還有一些空套房，我現在就幫您訂一間。）

✓ vacant（adj.）空著的、未被占用的

172

聆聽下列電話對談或語音，並將重點資訊填入空白劃線處。

① 🔊 MP3 **112**

A: Is this TS Airline? I'm Terry Sheldon calling to confirm my booking on the _____ flight to _____.

B: Oh, yes. Mr. Sheldon. We've received your booking, but I'm afraid that there were _____ _____ _____ in _____ class. I reserved a seat in _____ class for you, or you can also choose the _____ flight _____ hours later.

A: Well, I'll take _____ _____ flight, and don't forget I requested the _____ _____.

B: I'll book the _____ _____ for you right now, and make the note of your special meal as well.

② 🔊 MP3 **113**

A: Hello? This is Kevin Morris. I just left your restaurant _____ _____ _____ _____ and I can't find my _____ now. Could you check if I left it at my _____ or on _____ _____? I sat in the _____ _____ near the _____.

B: No problem, Mr. Morris. I'll ask our staff to check for you immediately. Maybe that will take some time. Is there any other way to reach you?

A: I really appreciate your help. Please call my wife's phone, _____.

B: Don't worry, sir. I'm sure it will turn up.

③ 🔊 MP3 **114**

This is the Wix computer product support line. All of our operators are _____ right now, but if you _____ on the line, we will assist you as soon as possible. If you are unable to wait and would like us to call you back, please press _____ to record _____, _____ _____, and the technical issue. If you would like to return to the _____ _____, please press _____. We thank you for your patience.

④ 🔊 MP3 **115**

Thank you for calling _____ _____. To inquire about a _____ _____, please press 1. To make an automated payment, please press _____. To make a _____ _____, please press _____. If you would like to speak with a loan officer or have other requests, please press _____.

⑤ 🔊 MP3 **116**

A: Hello, _____, this is Ronny, your _____ _____ _____.

B: Um … I'm afraid that you got the _____ number.

A: Oh, I'm sorry. Do you know Ruby Shelly?

B: No, I don't. Maybe she is a former _____ here. I just moved in _____ _____ ago.

A: Oh, I see. Again, I'm sorry to bother you.

Lesson 17

開會報告與討論

Part 1
要訣：會議的開場、報告與討論

開會時通常會有一個主持人以及多個報告者，最後會有討論及提問的時間。聆聽時，需要注意的部分有：在開頭要注意主持人的開場、開會的流程以及會議的重點，而報告中依據不同的報告類型會有不同的焦點，最後，提問討論也有常用的用語。

一、開場：介紹講者、流程大綱
二、報告：① 主要論點在最前與最後、② 兩種類型的報告
三、討論：表示是否認同或其他想法

Point 1 開場

會議的開場都會有一主持人先禮貌的歡迎來賓以及聽眾，再者就是介紹主講者並且公佈開會的流程。不像演講，開會為注重效率，形式很固定，所以聽者要把握開場的部分才能掌握開會的步調與重點。

Point 2 報告

1. 英文的報告都會將重點放在前面和最後面的結論處，結構上是：引言——中心論點——例證——結論。所以聽者要把握的就是最主要的論點部分。
2. 報告可以分為報告型與說服型，不同類型著重的特色當然也不同。
　→ 說服型：像推銷員般積極的使用情緒的字眼引導聽者

→ 報告型：像專家般使用平穩理智的例證說明事件

身為聆聽者，我們不需要太注意兩種類型的技巧，但是了解結構更可以捉住報告的重心。

Point 3　討論

　　會議最後會有開放討論的時間，通常每個人都會積極參與討論，注意表示意見的一些句子：

■ **I couldn't agree more.**

　　我不能同意你更多。（非常同意）

■ **I completely agree with you.**

　　我完全同意你。

■ **It's a very clear plan. I agree entirely.**

　　這是個很清楚的計畫。我完全同意。

■ **Co-operation is the best solution. You're right there.**

　　合作是最好的解決之道。你是對的。

■ **I agree with you up to a point, but I think you're going too far.**

　　我同意你提出的論點，但我覺得你有點離題了。

■ **I think expanding exports would be better.**

　　我認為拓展出口比較好。

■ **No, I can't agree with you, I'm afraid. I think it would be better to ...** 不，恐怕我不能同意你。我認為……會比較好。

■ **No, that's out of the question, I'm afraid. The price is far too high.** 不，恐怕這是完全不可能的了。這價格太高了。

　　有些人會表示不同意見，以下為意見表達常出現的句子，注意期間的轉折。

情境篇

I have an idea.

我有一個想法。

That's a great idea.

那是個好主意。

I don't like that idea.

我不喜歡那個主意。

How did you come up with your idea?

你怎麼會有這個想法？

Who came up with this idea?

誰想出這個主意的？

It was my idea. Why is she getting all the credit?

這是我的主意，但為何都是她得到功勞？

⊙ Part 2 ▸ 綜合範例

1 （A）開場 ◎ MP3 **117**

I would like to start by thanking all of you for coming today. The main purpose of this meeting is to set our targets for the rest of this year. The first thing we need to do is to review this year's performance. Then, we will look at the performance of individual staff members. Finally, I look forward to hearing your views on the future development of each department. I'd like each department to present its thoughts about these three areas and we will try to come up with some realistic goods together. Okay, who wants to be the first? Sales department, would you mind being first?

（我想要對你們今天的到來致謝。這場會議的目的是要為今年設定目標。首先我們要回顧今年目前為止的表現。接著我們來看一下個別員工們的表現。最後，我想要聽聽你們對各部門未來發展的看法。每個部門都要對三個區表示看法，然後我們可以試圖一起找出可行的目標。好了，誰要先？銷售部門，介意先發表嗎？）

會議開場的邏輯都會很清楚，重點（the main purpose of this meeting）也並不難抓。主講者一定會條理清楚地指出第一、第二、第三、最後，或是首先、然後、之後、最後等等，要不然就是用時間來顯示順序。

（B）報告

Hi, everyone, I'm Herbert Adams of the sales department. Last year, our staff had some success and earned twice as much sales revenue as we'd expected, but the first quarter of this year

was not as good because, as you know, our main competitor launched a popular new product. So the future development of our department is dependent on the products we have; that means that's your work, product development department. For our part, we would like the head office to give us more funds to retain our best salespeople.

（各位好，我是銷售部的 Herbert Adams。去年我們部門的員工做的很成功，收入達到了預期的兩倍。但是今年的第一季卻沒有比之前好，如你們所知，是因為我們的主要競爭對手有一個新的產品。所以我們部門的未來發展要倚靠我們有什麼產品，也就是說，那就是你們產品發展部的工作了。我們這邊呢，希望總公司能發給我們多一點的預算以留住最好的銷售人員。）

上述的報告雖然內容不多，仍有引言、例證、結論。引言說明之前做的很成功。例證一般會有數據，這裡只有提到比預期的兩倍還多（twice as much sales revenue）。結論是需要新產品以及多一點預算（funds）。除此之外，每一項論點都要有明確原因，如這裡所提的因為對方公司有新產品所以銷售變差，以及需要多一點預算是為了留住人才（retain our best salespeople）。

（C）討論

Mr. Adams, I agree that your department did a great job and has contributed a lot to the company, but about your last point, I think you're going too far. As you've said, we really need to provide something new for our customers, so the product development department also needs a large budget. Does anyone have other opinions?

（Adams 先生，我同意你們部門的確做的很好也替公司貢獻很多，但是你的最後一點，有點超過。就像你說的，我們需要提供新產品給消費者，所以產品發展部也需要更多預算。還有其他意見嗎？）

討論的部分沒有一定的規則模式，就是必須要表達出不同的意見才能達到開會的效果。不可能所有人都會同意某一件事，但提出否定意見也必須同時提出明確理由。

2 （A）開場 ◎ MP3 **118**

This meeting was requested by the Board of Directors. As you know, we have received many complaints about our service recently. Through the discussions today, we hope to gather some insights about how to solve these problems. In the first session, we'll have a 50-minute presentation by Grace Harbaugh from the customer service department to give you a better understanding of the complaints. After that, we'll have one hour to discuss solutions. Then, we'll recess for 20 minutes in the coffee lounge. After the break, we'll resume our meeting till noon. Now, let's turn our attention to Grace Harbaugh.

（這場會議是應董事會要求召開的。誠如你們所知，最近我們接到許多不滿我們服務的抱怨電話。透過今天的討論，我們希望能集結大家的看法來解決問題。第一部分，將由客戶服務部的 Grace Harbaugh 做一個 50 分鐘的簡報，讓我們對客訴情況有更深的了解。之後，我們會花一個小時來討論如何解決。然後大家可以在咖啡廳休息 20 分鐘。休息時間過後，我們繼續開會到中午。現在，讓我們把注意力轉向 Grace Harbaugh。）

✅ session（*n.*）開會

這場會議先是說明開會的目的，主要是要解決客戶抱怨的問題。 再來便是用許多時間相關的副詞或片語來呈現會議流程，如 in the first session、after that、then、after the break。

Good morning. I'm Grace from customer service. Since January, we've received 58 complaints. On average, two phone calls a day. 55% of the complaints were about shipment delays, 30% of them were about the damaged goods, and 10% of them were about the impoliteness of our carriers. Although we could place the blame for these mistakes on the terrible weather, the dissatisfaction of so many of our customers has seriously harmed our reputation.

（早安。我是客戶服務部的 Grace。自一月起，我們已經收到了 58 個抱怨。平均兩天會收到一通。55% 是抱怨貨物延遲到達，30% 是貨物毀損，10% 是因為沒禮貌的送貨員。雖然我們可以把錯誤都歸咎於惡劣的天氣，但這麼多客戶的不滿已經嚴重傷害我們的名譽。）

☑impoliteness（n.）粗魯、不禮貌的　☑dissatisfaction（n.）不滿
☑reputation（n.）名譽

這段報告用平穩理智的口吻提供許多數據化的例證，是屬報告型的簡報。

（C）討論

A: **This is really a crisis for us. How did our competitors handle the situation? They must have been affected by the snowstorms as well.**

B: **I heard that they were affected too, but we're the leading delivery company, and we were proud of it. We must do something.**

C: **How about making a commercial to apologize, or offering a discount?**

A: **Um … I don't like that idea. That will cost a lot. Our budget is not big enough.**

（A：這對我們而言真是一個危機。我們敵對陣營如何處理呢？他們一定也被
　　暴風雪影響。

　B：我聽說他們也有被影響，但我們一直是貨運的領導品牌，而且我們也引
　　以為傲。我們必須做些什麼。

　C：不如拍支廣告來道歉，或是給一點折扣？

　A：嗯……我不喜歡這個主意，這太花錢了。我們的經費不夠用。）

通常與會的人士都會參與意見，並盡量說出重點。

Part 3. 練習題 【詳解請見 p226】

會議的報告部分會因為不同領域而有專業的問題分析，本練習主要針對開場的重點、掌握討論時的表達為主。

第1題是會議開場的介紹，聆聽後請寫下會議的流程順序以及開會目的。

2-3 題分別是會議的開場以及之後的討論，聆聽後請寫下會議流程順序，以及討論的意見與支持與否的原因。

① 🔊 MP3 **119**

目的：＿＿＿＿＿＿＿＿＿＿＿＿＿＿＿＿＿＿＿＿＿＿＿＿＿＿

活動舉辦的時間 / 地點：＿＿＿＿＿＿＿＿＿＿＿＿＿＿＿＿＿

② 🔊 MP3 **120**

目的：＿＿＿＿＿＿＿＿＿＿＿＿＿＿＿＿＿＿＿＿＿＿＿＿＿＿

活動舉辦的時間：＿＿＿＿＿＿＿＿＿＿＿＿＿＿＿＿＿＿＿＿

③ 🔊 MP3 **121**

建議一：＿＿＿＿＿＿＿＿＿＿＿＿＿＿＿＿＿＿＿＿＿＿＿＿

是否被接受 / 原因：

＿＿＿＿＿＿＿＿＿＿＿＿＿＿＿＿＿＿＿＿＿＿＿＿＿＿＿＿

建議二：＿＿＿＿＿＿＿＿＿＿＿＿＿＿＿＿＿＿＿＿＿＿＿＿

是否被接受 / 原因：

＿＿＿＿＿＿＿＿＿＿＿＿＿＿＿＿＿＿＿＿＿＿＿＿＿＿＿＿

Lesson 18

上課聽講

Part 1.
要訣：聽講前的準備和做筆記技巧

上課聽講的內容通常都很長而且不時會出現專有名詞，在聆聽時會比較容易恍神，所以練習聽課堂講述內容時，必須要有做筆記的習慣。在此提供一些聽力及做筆記的技巧：

一、聆聽講課：事前預習、準備資料
二、筆記技巧：掌握重點、運用簡寫、課後複習

Point 1　聆聽講課

現場聽課時一定會聽到不認識的單字，首先切記不用因此而慌亂。要避免有太多字聽不懂，最好的辦法就是事先準備資料或事先將課堂會講到的內容預習看過一遍，將不熟悉的專有名詞先記下，並大聲念出來讓單字的音感留在腦裡，在聽課時就能反應更快。

Point 2　筆記技巧

作筆記要掌握快速且只記重點的原則。要快速必須要將某些常出現的字或長字用縮寫或特殊標記先代替，等到聽完課之後再做整理。要如何快速掌握重點，以下列出五種方法：

1. 黑板手寫的資訊或投影片的大綱

2. 重複提到的字

3. 上課時老師用重音或手勢語氣強調的，或分類成條目的單項

4. 課程最終結論時

5. 課程最初複習之前的概論

　　以上五種情形是一般重點會出現的地方，另外，在聽完課後必須儘快複習並把筆記中可能漏聽的地方補齊，日後要複習準備的時候就能完整的回憶重點資訊。

情境篇

1 ⦿ MP3 **122**

Vitamin C is an essential nutrient for humans and certain other animal species. It's an antioxidant that protects the body against oxidative stress. It is also a cofactor in at least eight enzymatic reactions including several collagen synthesis reactions that cause the most severe symptoms of scurvy when they are dysfunctional. (摘錄自 www.antioxidantchart.com)

（維他命 C 對人類以及其他某些動物而言是不可或缺的營養素。它是個可以防止身體老化的抗氧化劑，它也是個輔因子，可以和至少八種的酵素產生反應。這些反應包括一些膠原綜合體的作用。當作用不完全的時候會造成嚴重的壞血病症狀。）

⊘ nutrient（*n.*）營養物　⊘ antioxidant（*n.*）抗氧化劑　⊘ cofactor（*n.*）輔因子
⊘ enzymatic（*adj.*）酵素的　⊘ collagen（*n.*）膠原　⊘ synthesis（*n.*）綜合體
⊘ dysfunctional（*adj.*）不正常的

這可能會出現在醫學類型的課堂上。因為不同的科目會有不同的專有名詞，沒有預習或相關學術背景的人是很難聽懂的。尤其醫學類型的字非常多，一定要預習跟複習並要先將單字念出來熟記。對一般聽眾而言，至少可以從第一句標題句聽出主題：維他命 C 是不可或缺的營養素。

2 ⦿ MP3 **123**

The principal component of the Solar System is the Sun. Most large objects in orbit around the Sun lie near the plane of Earth's orbit, known as the ecliptic. All the planets and most other

objects <u>orbit</u> the Sun in the same direction: <u>counter-clockwise</u>, as viewed from above the Sun's north pole. There are <u>exceptions</u>, such as <u>Halley's</u> Comet. （摘錄自 Wikipedia, "Solar System"）

（太陽系主要的構成條件就是太陽。大部分的大型球體軌道都繞著太陽而行，也就是和地球的軌道（也就是我們熟知的黃道）相近。所有星球和大部分其他的球體繞太陽的軌道方向都是一樣的，也就是從太陽的北端來看是反時鐘方向的。也有例外，如哈雷彗星。）

☑component（*n.*）構成要素　☑solar system（*n.*）太陽系　☑orbit（*n.*）運行軌道
☑ecliptic（*n.*）黃道　☑counter-clockwise（*adj.*）逆時鐘方向的

同樣地，天文類型的單字也不簡單。除了預習複習和多唸以外，抓住開頭的主題句與最後結尾的結論是最好掌握的重點。這裡的主題句顯示重點在太陽系中的太陽。其他比較能聽懂的字也要把握，如反時鐘 counter-clockwise，就可猜到是說明軌道運行方向；例外 exceptions 就如哈雷彗星 Halley's Comet。其他的重點可能就要再聽下去才知道。

3 （◎）**MP3 124**

The <u>Renaissance</u> was a <u>cultural movement</u> that spanned roughly the <u>14th to the 17th</u> centuries, beginning in <u>Florence</u> in the <u>Late Middle Ages</u> and later spreading to the rest of Europe. The term is also generally used to refer to the <u>historical era</u>. To start, I want from each student a <u>ten-page report</u> detailing your ideas about the Renaissance, and listing any questions you have about it. Please have your report ready <u>by the next class</u>.

（改寫自 Wikipedia, "Renaissance"）

（文藝復興大致是個橫跨 14 到 17 世紀的文化運動。它開始於中古世紀晚期的佛羅倫斯，再散播到歐洲的其他地區。這個詞普遍被用來指稱為一個歷史性的時期。在開始之前，我要每個學生交一份 10 頁的報告詳述你對文藝復興的看法，並列出你的所有疑問，下堂課的時候要準備好。）

☑ Renaissance（*n.*）文藝復興　☑ pan（*v.*）橫跨、跨越

很明顯，這堂課的主題是 Renaissance 文藝復興，可以由第一句名詞解釋得知。時間、地名、和分類都是必須做筆記的重要資料。在國外，老師都會要求學生課前預習，尤其是希望學生能主動問問題，如此便更能在上課時進入狀況。還有，千萬別忘了要交的作業或考試資訊也是非常重要的聆聽重點。

4　🎧 MP3 125

Welcome to our film course in University of Paris VIII. My name is <u>Dr. Thomas Dickinson</u>, your teacher for this year's course. We're delighted to see the film tonight, _The 400 Blows by François Truffaut_—one of the great classics of <u>French New Wave Cinema</u>. In just a few minutes, we'll begin screening the film. After the film, I'll give a bit of background about the film, its director, and the history of <u>the French New Wave</u>, which left an indelible impact on world cinema. Now, let's enjoy the film.

You should each have received <u>a flyer</u> when you came in with a brief summary of what I'm going to discuss now. You should pay special attention now and review the material over the weekend, as you'll have <u>a quiz next Wednesday</u>. _The 400 Blows is a 1959 French film directed by François Truffaut_. One of the defining films of the <u>French New Wave</u>, it displays many of the characteristic traits of the movement. The <u>English title</u> is a direct translation of the French but <u>misses its meaning</u>, as the French title refers to the expression _faire les quatre cents coups_, which means "<u>to raise hell</u>." Some critics think the film covered <u>the topic of corporal punishment</u>. The film was <u>widely acclaimed</u>, winning numerous awards, including <u>the Best</u>

Director Award at the 1959 Cannes Film Festival and many other worldwide prizes. The New Wave was a <u>blanket term</u> coined by critics for <u>a group of French filmmakers of the late 1950s and 1960s</u> who were <u>influenced by Italian Neorealism and classical Hollywood</u> <u>cinema.</u>（改寫自 Wikipedia, "The 400 Blows"）

（歡迎來到第八學院的電影課程，我的名字是 Thomas Dickinson 教授，你們今年的授課老師。今天晚上很高興能來看看這部電影，法蘭西斯‧楚浮的四百擊，法國新浪潮的偉大經典之一。幾分鐘之後，我們就要開始看這部電影。看完之後，我會講一些電影的相關背景、它的導演、還有法國新浪潮的歷史，這可是對世界電影有很深的影響。現在，我們先來欣賞這部電影吧。）

你們每個人在進來時應該都有拿到一張單子，上面有我準備要討論的內容大綱。你們現在應該要專心聽然後周末要複習，因爲下個星期三會有小考。四百擊是楚浮 1959 年拍的法國電影，它是法國新浪潮著名的電影之一，其中含有許多該運動的特徵。英文標題是直譯法文但卻遺失它原有的含義；法文標題 *faire les quatre cents coups* 表現出「將地獄升起」的含義。許多批評家認爲這部電影包含了體罰這個主題。這部電影廣泛的受到讚揚，得了無數的獎，包括 1959 年坎城影展的對佳導演和許許多多國際性的獎。新浪潮是個概括的詞，是評論家用以指稱在 1950 到 1960 年間的一群受義大利新寫實主義及古典好萊塢電影影響的法國電影拍攝者。

✅characteristic（*adj.*）獨特的　✅trait（*n.*）特徵　✅corporal（*adj.*）肉體的
✅acclaim（*v.*）歡呼、稱讚

這是一堂電影史的課，學生課前就會知道該堂課會放映法國新浪潮導演楚浮的電影「四百擊」。這段講課比較長一些，但沒有太多專有名詞，聽聽看，根據重複的字，以及一些數字或名詞，試著做出筆記，聽完後再來看劃線的重點。

Part 3. **練習題** 【詳解請見 p227】

題目一開始會先提供大概的課堂種類，有心理準備後，聆聽並盡量多做一些筆記，再選出何為該講課內容的主題。

🔊 MP3 **126**

① **Chernobyl Nuclear Power Plant**

_____ Which is the topic of the section?

A: The influence to the residents of Pripyat

B: The seriousness of the radiation poisoning

C: The reasons of the explosion

🔊 MP3 **127**

② **Birth Order**

_____ Which statement is true?

A: Many people don't agree to the theory of birth order.

B: The first child is more social and good at negotiation.

C: The birth order will effect whether a person's job is good or not.

🔊 MP3 **128**

③ **Psychology**

_____ Which statement is true?

A: Psycology's goal is to understand human being's development.

B: Psychologists study people's mental illness.

C: Psychology is a science.

④ Science Fiction

_____ Which statement is true?

A: Science fiction is about the past and our world.

B: Readers might feel that such things in the stories could be real.

C: Steven King is a scientist as well as a science fiction writer.

Lesson 19

電視節目

 # Part 1.
要訣：從電視節目練習日常用語

　　從電視節目中練習當地的日常生活用語以及語言運用方式是最直接且實用的。跟閱讀文章不同，電視節目中的內容用字不會太艱澀，對話上也和文法教科書上的大不相同。電視節目的種類很多，舉凡戲劇、新聞、談話、綜藝以及知識類都可以做成電視節目，前面章節已將新聞單獨列出，所以以下介紹知識、戲劇和綜藝三種類型節目：

一、社會議題或科學新知
二、情境劇
三、綜藝或益智節目

Point 1　社會議題或科學新知

　　雖然討論的主題可能很嚴肅或專業，電視節目中的討論者在一開頭介紹主題時，不會像文章般一開始便點出主題句，而會有一小段日常生活的小故事或輕鬆感人的開場白。相較之前的情境，電視節目中講述的內容比新聞或講課來的簡單。

◎ MP3 **130**

1 If I want to protect myself, I can use a knife, or maybe a gun. But, how can animals defend themselves? A lion? Nobody will worry about his safety, but how about a plant-eating animal?

What kind of the defenses does the Malayan Tapir have? The Malayan Tapir is black and white. Cats see only in black and white, so the Malayan Tapir's colors make them invisible to their main predator, large cats. （改寫自 Discovery 頻道）

（如果我要保護自己，我可以用刀或槍，但動物要如何防衛呢？獅子？沒有人會擔心他的安全吧？但那草食性動物呢？馬來貘要用什麼方式防衛呢？馬來貘是黑色跟白色的，而貓科動物只能看到白色和黑色，所以馬來貘的顏色可以使自己在主要天敵貓科動物眼中變隱形。）

☑ defend（v.）防禦　　☑ Malayan Tapir（n.）馬來貘

☑ invisible（adj.）看不見的　　☑ predator（n.）食肉動物、掠奪者

....

這段話的主題是在介紹馬來貘的膚色及其功能，但在之前會先用其他生活化的方式引導聽者進入主題。

◎ MP3 131

2 I think most people believe that science will never answer the most important questions in human life. Questions like: "What's worth living for?" "What's worth dying for?" "What constitutes a good life?"

（我想大部分的人都認為科技無法回答人類生活中最重要的問題，例如「什麼值得我們活著？」、「什麼值得我們去死？」或「是什麼組成一個好的生活？」）

☑ constitute（v.）構成

....

這段開場白用一些我們平常都可能會想到的問題來質疑科技，然而主講者的重點其實是科技可以回答一些抽象的問題，但在開始分析之前，講者會先用簡單的方式先吸引聽者去思考，而且這樣也比較有趣一些。

196

◎ MP3 **132**

　　電視情境劇是英美現在流行的連續劇型態，每集都會有一個主題。在這類型的戲劇節目中，角色間的對話都是簡短且詼諧的，和我們一般在教科書中學到的制式的對話模式完全不同，而是跳躍式的，我們必須要用較多的聯想力才能感受到其中的幽默。

1 A: How's your life before marriage?

B: I'm not married.

A: Oh! For some reason, I thought you had like three kids.

B: No! Never married! No kids.

A: 'Cause sometimes you have like some food stains on your shirts and stuff….

A：妳婚前的生活如何？

B：我沒有結婚。

A：喔！有些原因讓我認為你有差不多三個小孩了。

B：不！從沒結婚！沒有小孩！

A：因為有時候你的襯衫或衣服上都有食物的汙漬…

（改編自 30 Rocks）

　　這類型的對話並不會按照我們學校學的教科書上的一問一答，而是繞著一個主題的跳躍式的對談。如最後一句表示為何 A 會以為 B 已經結婚有小孩的原因，但是乍聽之下可能不能馬上聯想到，而且整段對話主要的重點在最後才點出：some food stains on your shirts，取笑 B 是個生活整潔有問題的未婚女子。

通常綜藝節目都像是聊天一般，字不會難，但說的會比較快。因為都是以表演或其他主題為主，說話的內容只是串場用的，功能性居多，聽不懂也可以猜的出來。

◎ MP3 **133**

1 Welcome back to "American New Stars." Now the judges' cards have been collected, and we'll announce of the top ten finalists live. But before that, let's see a special video reviewing our candidates' prior performances. The first one, Pia Toscano.

（改寫自 American Idol 節目 ,2011.）

（歡迎回來「美國新星」，現在評審們的分數卡已經收齊，我們將現場直播，宣布前十名。但在這之前，我們來看看特別錄製的影片，複習一下我們候選者之前的表演。第一位，Pia Toscano！）

這是最近流行的實境秀 Reality Show 的模擬片段，主持人需要介紹表演者、詢問評審意見、以及帶動氣氛等等，綜藝類型裡，主持人最需要說話，但其實都是屬於功能性的。

◎ MP3 **134**

2 Host A: Let's welcome our next candidate, Max Ford, a naval pilot from Virginia Beach. (applause) Ok! You are really a handsome guy, wow! I thought the flight officers were the most handsome. Now I'm changing my mind. We don't have much time, so are you ready to play? You know the rules?

Candidate: Ok! Yes, I'm ready.

Host B:　　OK, Let's play "Millionaire." (applause) Number one, in golf, scoring one stroke under par on a hole is called a what? A: Doggie B: Duckie C: Birdie D: Miracle（改寫自 Millionaire 節目, 2009）

（主持人 A：歡迎我們下一個參賽者，Max Ford，一個來自 Virginia Beach 的海軍軍官。（鼓掌）哇！你真是個帥哥！我以為空軍軍官最帥，我現在改變想法了。我們沒有很多時間，所以，你準備好要玩了嗎？你知道規則吧？參賽者：好的，我準備好了。主持人 B：好！我們來進行「百萬富翁」（鼓掌）第一題，高爾夫運動，以低於標準桿一桿的成績打進洞稱為什麼？A：多吉　B：得奇　C：柏蒂　D：奇蹟）

主持人除了要掌控節目流程，保持順暢，也需要確保錄影氣氛愉快，所以一定會跟來賓閒聊。內容就如同一般民眾打招呼閒話家常，所以不會難懂。比較難懂的專有字，節目也會打上字幕。

情境篇

Part 2. 練習題 【詳解請見 p230】

請聆聽並抓出重點，找出所要表達的主要含意並回答問題。

① 🔊 MP3 135

What do you think is the main focus in this talk?

_____

② 🔊 MP3 136

According to the program, why is Hong Kong the best travel destination in Asia?

(1) _____

(2) _____

(3) _____

(4) _____

③ 🔊 MP3 137

_____ What is the key point of this dialogue?

A: The man proposed to the woman.

B: Joey proposed to the woman.

C: The woman is going to engage.

④ 🔊 MP3 138

_____ Does the man have a sarcasm sign?

A: Yes, he does.

B: No, this is also sarcasm.

C: Maybe. We don't know.

解答篇

Listening

Listening

❶ Just go down Market Road / for two blocks / and turn left.

（就沿著 Market Road 走兩個街區然後左轉。）

❷ Sometimes / she sits by the window / looking at the flowers / in the garden.

（她有時坐在窗邊看著花園裡的花。）

❸ The doctor says that / it is impossible for her / to go to school today.

（醫生說她今天不可能去學校。）

❹ There's a pretty good / barber shop / near my house.

（有個不錯的理髮院在我家附近。）

❺ The kid is holding / his bicycle seat / and handle bars.

（這孩子正握著他的腳踏車座椅跟把手。）

❻ The most convenient way / to get around this small town / is to ride a bike.

（周遊這個小鎮最方便的方式就是騎單車了。）

❼ The patient responds verbally / or with gestures / to indicate emotions /such as pain, / stress / or anxiety.

（病人用話語或手勢回應來表達情緒，如痛苦、壓力、或焦慮。）

⊘gesture（*n.*）手勢　⊘anxiety（*n.*）焦慮

❽ He and five other boys / took turns / jumping rope / for two and half hours / and collected more than US$1,200 / in donations / for the American Heart Association.

（他和其他五位男孩輪流跳繩兩個半小時並收集了超過 1200 美金以捐贈給美國心臟協會。）

⊘jump rope（*v.*）跳繩　⊘donation（*n.*）捐獻　⊘association（*n.*）協會

❾ In ancient Egypt, / as long ago as 1500 BC, / outward appearance / expressed a person's status, / role in society, / and political position.

（西元前 1500 年，在古埃及外表顯示一個人的身份、在社會裡的角色階級和政治地位。）

⊘ancient（*adj.*）古老的　⊘outward（*adj.*）外表的　⊘status（*n.*）地位、身分

⊘position（*n.*）地位、位置

❿ We have had / plenty of rain / so far / this year, / so there should be / an abundant supply / of fresh water / this summer.

（我們今年有很多雨量，所以這個夏天的新鮮水應該有充分的供給量。）

○abundant (*adj.*) 大量的 ○supply (*n.*) 供給

⑪ The crimes, / like the one / that was committed / in northern Cambodia / today, / are aimed at sowing enmity / between our citizens.

（今天在北柬埔寨所犯下的這個罪行主要是要在我們居民中散播敵意。）

○crime (*n.*) 罪 ○commit (*v.*) 犯罪 ○aim (*v.*) 瞄準 ○sow (*v.*) 播種

○enmity (*n.*) 敵意 ○citizen (*n.*) 市民

⑫ Beginning with Toy Story in 1995, / Pixar has produced eleven feature films, / all of which / have met with critical / and commercial success.

（從 1995 年的 Toy Story 開始，Pixar 已經出產了 11 部劇情電影，全部的作品都有評論及商業上的成功。）

○feature film (*n.*) 劇情片 ○critical (*adj.*) 評論性的

○commercial (*adj.*) 商業性的

⑬ Flags on all regional buildings / will fly at half-staff / and all entertainment programs on local TV / will be cancelled / as well as concerts / and theater performances.

（所有當地大樓都會降半旗而且所有當地電視台的娛樂節目也將取消，音樂會與戲院表演也一樣。）

○regional (*adj.*) 地區的 ○entertainment (*n.*) 娛樂

⑭ As of 2010, / this film, / it could be said, / was the most successful film / in history.

（至 2010 年為止，這部電影可以說是影史上最成功的。）

⑮ A girl / with her own views / will perhaps be able to / more quickly / and effectively / solve life's problems.

（一個有主見的女性或許更能迅速有效率地解決自己的人生難題。）

○effectively (*adv.*) 有效地

Lesson 2　參考解答與翻譯

❶ As opportunities in Asia grow, so will Eastline's ways of getting you there.

（當亞洲的機會成長，東方航空的路線也會帶你到那裡。）

❷ Have you ever cooked chicken on the grill?

（你有烤過雞嗎？）

○grill (*v.*) 烤

❸ You are going on vacation, aren't you?
（你要去度假，是嗎？）

❹ In your opinion, what kind of printer should we buy?
（以你的意見，我們該買哪種印表機？）

❺ When will the boss be able to arrange to meet us, then?
（那麼老闆將會何時抽空見我們呢？）
☑ arrange（v.）安排

❻ How can I get to the hotel from the airport?
（我要怎麼從機場到旅館呢？）

❼ Couldn't you possibly give us a more specific suggestion?
（你有可能再給我們具體一點的建議嗎？）
☑ specific（adj.）特定的

❽ His company is located on the 27th floor, office 27G.
（他的公司位在 27 樓 27G 室。）

❾ Should I get the blue one?
（我應該拿藍色的嗎？）

❿ While he was swimming in the sea, his mother just stood by watching him.
（當他正在海裡游泳時，他媽媽就只是站在一邊看著他。）

⓫ Pack now and get ready to be COOL!
（現在快打包，然後準備「酷」一下！）

⓬ Worried about catching a cold? You don't have to be.
（擔心著涼？你不需要。）

⓭ Kelly: Have you read the news about the Cine Prize nominations?
Eunice: Yeah. I can't believe _Took Off_ got the most nominations. It's not that good.
（Kelly：你有看到關於 Cine 獎的提名新聞嗎？
Eunice：有啊，我真不敢相信 _Took Off_ 得到最多提名。它沒有那麼棒。）
☑ nomination（n.）提名

⓮ Last month, a hacker who identified himself as "Gabriel" claimed to have broken into the computer system of the British publisher of _Harry Potter_.

（上個月，有個自稱是"加百列"的駭客宣稱他侵入了出版哈利波特的英國出版社的電腦系統。）

☑hacker（*n.*）駭客　☑identify（*v.*）認同　☑claim（*v.*）聲稱

⑮ As thousands of new immigrants from Southeastern Asia have moved to Taiwan for work or marriage, we should try our best to help them adjust to our society.

（當上千名來自東南亞的新移民來台灣工作或結婚，我們應該盡力幫助他們適應我們的社會。）

☑immigrant（*n.*）移民　☑adjust（*v.*）適應

Lesson 3　參考解答與翻譯

＊說明：本課解答中的 ▨ 灰底處為口語省略讀法。

❶ Do *ya* like the Internet?

（你喜歡網路嗎？）

❷ *She'ad* finished *er* homework at 8:00.

（她已在八點完成她的作業。）

❸ There's a room *fer* children-n-babies.

（有一間給嬰幼兒的房間。）

❹ Do ya want a yellow coat-*er* a red one?

（你要黃色還是紅色的外套？）

❺ Why*'as* she gone *tu* New York?

（他為何去紐約？）

❻ I musta been crazy *da* try *da* find *'is* house out here.

（我一定是瘋了才會試著在這找到他的房子。）

❼ *Whacha gonna* do that for?

（你做那個是為了什麼？）

❽ *Why're ya doin'* this now? *Ya shoulda* done it a few days ago.

（你現在為什麼要做這個？好幾天前你就應該要做了。）

❾ A: Hello! *Whaddaya* been *doin* lately? B: Oh, I've been *hikin* a lot. So, where as *yer* sister been? I haven't seen *er*.

（A：你好！你最近在做些什麼？ B：喔！我做很多健行活動。那麼，你姊妹都在哪？我都沒看到她。）

⑩ A: *Whadda* we need-*du* buy? B: Well, a couple *a* bottles *a* water, some sandwitches-*n*-chocolate…Wait! I don't have my credit card. Do *ya* have *yers*?

（A：我們需要買什麼？ B：嗯，幾瓶水、一些三明治，還有巧克力。等等！我沒有帶我的信用卡，你有嗎？）

⑪ Life is like a box *a* chocolates. You never know what *yer gonna* get.

（生命就像一盒巧克力，你永遠不知道你將會拿到哪一個。）

⑫ She*'s* worried about this document *get'in* there late.

（她擔心這個文件會遲到。）

⑬ *Yer* really crazy to go *swim'in（in 省略）* the lake on a cold winter day. *Don't-cha* feel cold?

（你真的很瘋狂，居然在這麼冷的冬天在湖裡游泳。你都不覺得冷嗎？）

⑭ What am I *gonna* do? I don't even know *what's happen'in* right now.

（我該做什麼？我根本不知道現在發生什麼事？）

⑮ *I've loved-ja* more than *I've* ever loved any *woman-n-I've* waited *fe* you longer than *I've* ever waited *fer* any woman.

（我愛你勝過我曾愛過的任何女人，我等著你也久過我等的所有女人。）

Lesson 4 | 參考解答與翻譯

❶ Why does your roommate think he should look for a cheaper apartment?

（為什麼你的室友認為他需要去找一個更便宜的公寓？）

❷ I apologize for coming late to the meeting this morning.

（我為我今早會議遲到致歉。）

☑ apologize（*v.*）道歉

❸ The turtle is the animal my sister is most afraid of. She cries and runs away even when she sees a picture of one.

（烏龜是我姐妹最怕的動物。即使是看到它的照片，她都會哭著逃跑。）

❹ Nature can color our everyday lives with lovely surprises.

（大自然可以用些美好的驚喜為我們的日常生活妝點色彩。）

❺ Mom, thank you for everything you've done for Tim and me.

（媽，謝謝你為我和 Tim 所做的每一件事。）

⑥ Happy Puppy is a relatively new service.

（Happy Puppy 是個很新的服務。）

⑦ If you had listened carefully, this accident never would have happened.

（如果你有仔細聽，這個意外就永遠不會發生了。）

⑧ This lecture will definitely produce an exciting debate.

（這個演講一定將會引起精彩的討論。）

✓lecture（*n.*）講座　✓debate（*n.*）辯論

⑨ Please exercise caution and read all safety instructions before use.

（請小心使用，並在使用前閱讀所有安全注意事項。）

✓safety instruction（*n.*）安全指南

⑩ It is highly recommended for those who plan to go to graduate school.

（這個是高度推薦給計畫要讀研究所的人。）

✓recommend（*v.*）推薦

⑪ Ms. Li's business expanded very quickly.

（Li 女士的生意擴張的非常快。）

⑫ As a health editor, I am often inundated by information about the latest disease, the newest cure, the healthiest diet, or the best exercise.

（身為健康版的編輯，我經常被最近的疾病、最新的治療方法、最健康的減肥方式或最棒的運動等資訊給淹沒。）

✓inundate（*v.*）如洪水般撲來

⑬ The young Taiwanese pianist performed remarkably well and won the first prize in the music competition.

（這個年輕的台灣鋼琴家表演的非常出色並贏得音樂比賽第一名。）

✓perform（*v.*）表演　✓remarkably（*adv.*）顯著地

⑭ Can you see what the word is? The first letter is not clear.

Oh, it's "r." The word is "ring."

（A：你看的出來這個字是什麼嗎？第一個字母不清楚。 B：喔！是 r。這個字是 ring。）

⑮ A: Here's the order: Williams, Smith, Lewis, and Jones. Yes, Lewis?

B: I want to go last.

A: I've already decided. The sequence is fixed.

解答篇

（A：順序如下：威廉斯、史密斯、路易斯、還有瓊斯。路易斯，什麼事？B：我想要最後。
A：我已經決定好了，次序沒辦法改變。）

☑ sequence（*n.*）次序

Lesson 5 | 參考解答與翻譯

① didn't

② hasn't

③ shouldn't

④ not

⑤ no

⑥ can't

⑦ nothing

⑧ seldom

⑨ rarely

⑩ hardly

⑪ scarcely

⑫ seldom

⑬ Don't, Don't

⑭ wouldn't

⑮ wasn't, weren't

【參考翻譯】

① 我不是有意要傷害你。

② 她還沒收到我的郵件。

③ 畢竟，機器不應該比人重要。

④ 我不確定我們明天是否還能去釣魚。

⑤ 我對烹飪沒有興趣所以我總是請我兄弟替我料理。

⑥ 我無法想像這水裡之前曾有魚。

⑦ 除了沙子我什麼都沒看到。

⑧ Sandy 很少在上午八點之前起床。

⑨ 雖然他是廚師，Reberto 幾乎不料理他自己的餐點。

⑩ 他太忙了以至於很難跟他的家人吃晚餐。

⑪ Jason 在車禍中嚴重受傷，他幾乎無法移動他的腿並且立刻被送到醫院。

⑫ 這種動物很少被看到，因為它活在 4,000 公尺海底而且很難被找到。

⑬ 你別那樣，你別說道別的話。

⑭ 如果他在做之前跟我說，我現在就不會這麼生氣。

⑮ 雖然他們在做的化學實驗不困難，但他們無法得到有用的資料。

Lesson 6 | 參考解答與翻譯

① Cheese, / powdered milk, / and yogurt / are common milk products.

（起司、奶粉和優格是普遍的奶製品。）

☑ powdered milk（*n.*）奶粉

❷ We are completely devoted to helping dogs / enjoy a full and active life.
（我們完全致力於幫助狗兒享受完整又活潑的生活。）

❸ This new computer is obviously superior to the old one / because it has many new functions.
（這個新電腦很明顯地優於舊的因為它有許多新功能。）
  ⓥ superior to（*ph.*）優於

❹ Sally, / a junior high school student, / would like to go to the Big Dream Summer Camp.
（Sally，一個國中生，想要去大夢想夏令營。）

❺ Do you have all your figures ready / for the auditors / who are coming in?
（那個正走來的查帳員要查的數據你都準備好了嗎？）
  ⓥ figure（*n.*）數字金額

❻ Did you get into trouble / for getting home late / from our date?
（我們約會後讓你很晚回家，有帶給你任何麻煩嗎？）

❼ Under the leadership of newly elected president Barack Obama, / the US is expected to turn a new page / in its history.
（在新選出的總統 Barak Obama 領導下，美國被期許邁向歷史嶄新的一頁。）
  ⓥ leadership（*n.*）統御力　ⓥ elected（*adj.*）當選的

❽ I really don't believe that / Kevin can complete the job, even with the help of the new assistant.
（我真的不相信 Kevin，即使有新助理幫忙，能完成這份工作。）

❾ Because of the high levels of air pollution, / officials decided / it was not the right time to reduce the vehicle tax.
（因為空氣污染的緣故，官員決定現在不是個降低汽車稅的好時機。）

❿ To live an efficient life, / we have to arrange the things to do / in order of priority and start with the most important ones.
（要過一個有效率的生活，我們必須將事情排列優先順序並從最重要的開始。）
  ⓥ priority（*n.*）優先

⓫ She was about to call 911 again / when the intruder managed to stand up / with David clinging to his back.

（David 緊抓著闖入者的背，而闖入者正準備站起來時，她差不多要再打一次 911 報警電話。）

☑intruder（*n.*）闖入者　☑manage（*v.*）設法做到　☑cling（*v.*）緊握不放

⑫ According to many observers, / the Hollywood movie star George Clooney / played a pivotal role in Sudan's historic referendum.

（根據許多觀察者，好萊塢電影明星 George Clooney 在蘇丹歷史性的公民投票扮演很重要的角色。）

☑observer（*n.*）觀察者　☑pivotal（*adj.*）中樞的　☑referendum（*n.*）公民投票

⑬ What was most touching and encouraging for me / was to see farmers, / even beggars donating / and doing their part.

（對我來說最感動和激勵的是看到農夫或甚至是乞討者來捐獻並獻出一己之力。）

☑touching（*adj.*）感人的　☑encouraging（*adj.*）激勵人心的　☑beggar（*n.*）乞討者

⑭ Most Americans believe that / human trafficking happens everywhere / but in their country.

（大多數的美國人都相信非法販賣人口在各地都有發生，但就不發生在他們自己的國家。）

☑trafficking（*n.*）非法交易

⑮ Twisted every way, / what answer can I give? / Am I to risk my life to win the chance to live? / Can I betray the man who once inspired my voice? / Do I become his prey? / Do I have any choice?

（無論如何都被糾纏，我能給什麼答案？我要冒險去求得生存的機會嗎？我能背叛那個曾啟發我歌聲的人嗎？我成為他的獵物了嗎？我能有任何選擇嗎？）

☑twist（*v.*）扭轉　☑risk（*v.*）冒風險　☑inspire（*v.*）啟發　☑prey（*n.*）俘虜

Lesson 7 　參考解答與翻譯

❶ Are you alright?

（你還好嗎？）

❼ She didn't attend the meeting, did she?

（她沒有參加這個會議，對吧？）

❸ What service does this company offer?

（這家公司提供的是什麼服務？）

❹ Aren't you supposed to be in class now?

（你現在不是應該要在上課嗎？）

☑ supposed (*adj.*) 假定的

❺ Do you mind my smoking here?

（你介意我在這裡抽菸嗎？）

❻ When will Tom be able to complete this project?

（Tom 何時能夠完成這項計畫？）

❼ Is it true you put in for a transfer to London?

（你真的申請調職到倫敦嗎？）

☑ transfer (*v.*) 搬遷、轉換

❽ Would you like to go swimming with me?

（你想要跟我一起去游泳嗎？）

❾ How do these people feel about the television sets?

（這些人覺得這些電視機組如何呢？）

❿ Why are you so stupid?

（你為什麼這麼笨？）

⓫ Could you give me a hand?

（你可以幫我嗎？）

⓬ Could you leave the door open a little, Sarah?

（你可以留一點門縫嗎，Sarah？）

⓭ What is the main purpose of the announcement?

（這個公告的主要目的是什麼？）

⓮ Henry, don't you think fishing is boring? You just sit by the water and wait all day long.

（Henry，你不覺得釣魚很無趣嗎？你就只是坐在水邊然後等一整天。）

⓯ A: Based on the weather report, when will sun rise?

B: You've asked me more than ten times. Be patient, okay?

（A：根據氣象報告，太陽哪時會升起？ B：你已經問我超過十遍了。耐心點，好嗎？）

Lesson 8　參考解答與翻譯

❶ Many people like to drink bottled water because they feel that tap water may not be safe, but is bottled water really any better?

（許多人喜歡喝瓶裝水因為他們覺得自來水不安全，但，瓶裝水真的比較好嗎？）

■ 質疑瓶裝水的安全。

❷ If the weather is fine this weekend, my family will go to the beach for three days.

（如果這個周末天氣好，我們家將會去海邊三天。）

■ 家人周末要去海邊的條件與資訊。

❸ A: How about going to the cafeteria?

B: It's too crowded.

（A：去吃自助餐好嗎？ B：太擠了。）

✓cafeteria (*n.*) 自助餐廳

■ 去自助餐廳的意願與否及原因。

❹ The islands have an average temperature of 80 degrees, so don't forget your shorts and swimsuits.

（島嶼的氣溫平均為華氏 80 度，別忘記帶短褲跟泳衣。）

■ 島嶼天氣熱所以要帶適合的穿著。

❺ A: Excuse me, when are the departures for Chicago today?

B: Nine and ten o'clock, twelve- fifteen, two forty-five, and four-thirty.

（A：請問，今天啓程去芝加哥的時間？ B：9 點、10 點、12 點 15、2 點 45 和 4 點半。）

✓departure (*n.*) 離開啓程

■ 去芝加哥班次的時間資訊。

❻ Due to poor weather conditions, all flights departing for New York will be postponed until further notice.

（往紐約的班機因天候不佳，直到進一步消息宣布前，將全面延後飛行。）

✓postpone (*v.*) 延後

■ 去紐約班機延宕的原因。

❼ Scientists discovered that eating plenty of pizza seems to lower the risk of cancer. The protective ingredient is tomato sauce.

（科學家發現吃大量的 pizza 可以降低患癌的危險。具有保護功能的食材是番茄醬。）

✓cancer (*n.*) 癌症　✓protective (*adj.*) 保護的　✓ingredient (*n.*) 原料

■ 吃披薩降低癌症的原因在於番茄醬。

❽ The annual Comic-Con conference is becoming more well-known as more major motion pictures that are being made now are based on comic book properties.

（年度動漫節越來越廣為人知，因為現在有更多重要電影都是根據漫畫而製成的。）

☑properties（*n.*）特性

■ Comic-Con 的名稱和漫畫以及電影有關。

❾ In television, the cancelled show is a common thing. Audience tastes are hard to predict, so every network is bound to produce its share of losers as well as winners.

（在電視節目中，節目被停播是很一般的。觀眾的品味很難被預測，所以每家電視公司都會製作失敗的作品就如同製作成功的節目一樣多。）

☑bound to（*ph.*）一定會

■ 失敗的電視節目和成功的電視節目一樣平常

❿ When it gets hot outside, everyone starts obsessing over ice cream sandwiches. Not me. Instead, I want to talk about savory, greasy, fried grilled cheese sandwiches.

（當外面天氣變熱，每個人都被冰淇淋三明治吸引；但不是我。我反而想談談美味油膩的烤起司三明治。）

☑obsess（*v.*）著迷　　☑instead（*adv.*）取而代之的　　☑savory（*adj.*）美味的

☑greasy（*adj.*）油膩的

■ 熱天作者不受冰淇淋誘惑卻選擇烤起司三明治。

Lesson 9　參考解答與翻譯

❶（人物描述──Duncan）

Duncan, 47, with long gray hair, was called the mother of modern dance because she brought lots of new ideas into the dancing of her time.

Duncan，47 歲，留著長灰色的頭髮，被稱為是現代舞蹈之母，因為她將許多新思想帶進她那年代的舞蹈。

❷（景物描述──北極光）

The northern lights look different every time you see them. They dance in the sky, changing all the time. The light is often seen as arcs, clouds, or streaks. The most common color you see is green, though the lights can be purple or red as well.

北極光每次你在不同時間看都會不一樣。它們在天空跳舞，總是在變化。那光看起來時常會像弧形、雲朵狀或條紋狀。你最常見的顏色是綠色，雖然也可能是紫色或紅色。

解答篇

❸（物品描述──錶）

This elegant gentlemen's timepiece features a classic, round-shaped case, a silver dial and a black strap. Water resistant to 50 meters. Two-year international warranty.

這個典雅的男錶，採用經典圓形錶殼，搭配銀色錶盤及黑色錶帶。50 米防水功能。附兩年國際保固。

☑timepiece（*n.*）鐘、錶、計時器 ☑dial（*n.*）刻度盤 ☑strap（*n.*）帶子
☑resistant（*adj.*）抵抗的、防⋯⋯的 ☑warranty（*n.*）保證書

❹（物品描述──牛仔褲）

This pair of 1969 mid-weight skinny boot jeans with light blue wash costs $69.95, but is now on sale for only $45.

這件 1969 年經典刷淡藍色緊身喇叭牛仔褲價值 69.95 元，現在特價 45 元。

❺（物品描述──沙發床）

Sofa beds are a very popular type of furniture, specially designed to solve problems in modern homes. A sofa bed looks like a sofa or a couch but can be easily transformed into a bed. The size of a standard sofa bed is 35 × 79 inches.

沙發床是非常流行的家具形態，特別設計給現代家庭解決問題。沙發床看似沙發椅但也可以輕易變成床鋪。標準沙發床的大小是 35×79 吋。

❻（人物描述──畢卡索）

Pablo Picasso, born on October 25, 1881, was a Spanish painter who lived most of his life in France. He is widely known for his revolutionary artistic accomplishments, which made him one of the best-known figures in 20th century art.

Pablo Picasso 生於 1881 年 10 月 25 日，是個西班牙畫家但他一生大都住在法國。他因他的革命性藝術貢獻廣泛為人所知，這也讓他成為 20 世紀藝術界最有名的人物之一。

☑revolutionary（*adj.*）革命的 ☑accomplishment（*n.*）成就

❼（物品描述──費城）

Philadelphia is located in the Northeastern United States. It is the fifth-most-populous city in the United States, with a 2010 U.S. Census estimated population of 1,526,006. Philadelphia is also the commercial, cultural, and educational center of the Delaware Valley.（節錄自 http://en.wikipedia.org/wiki/Philadelphia）

費城位於美國東北，是美國人口第五多的都市，2010 年美國人口統計估計有 1,526,006 人。它也是 Delaware Valley 的商業、文化和教育中心。

☑ estimate（*v.*）估計　☑ population（*n.*）人口

⑧（人物描述——哈利波特）

Harry Potter, an orphan with a lightning-shaped scar on his forehead, discovers at the age of eleven that he is a wizard. Harry becomes a student at Hogwarts School of Witchcraft and Wizardry. He then learns to overcome the problems that face him, including magical, social and emotional ones. The greatest test for him is his fight with the Dark Lord Voldemort.

（改寫自 http://en.wikipedia.org/wiki/Harry_Potter）

Harry Potter 的前額有著閃電形狀的疤痕，他是個孤兒，在 11 歲時發現自己是個魔法師。Harry 成為霍格華茲魔法與巫術學院的學生。接著他學習去克服接踵而至的難題，包括魔法、社交、和情緒上的問題。最大的考驗就是要與黑魔王佛地魔戰鬥。

☑ scar（*n.*）疤痕　☑ forehead（*n.*）額頭　☑ orphan（*n.*）孤兒　☑ wizard（*n.*）巫師
☑ witchcraft（*n.*）巫術、魔法　☑ wizardry（*n.*）巫術、魔法

Lesson 10　參考解答與翻譯

❶ We cautiously walk along a wooden platform. Then, after turning a corner, we're bombarded with pods of fireflies.（改寫自 Arthur Conan Doyle's The Lost World）

我們小心地沿著木製的平台行走，然後，轉過一個轉角後，我們被一群螢火蟲砲轟攻擊。

❷ It was evening, their children were asleep in the back seat. Suddenly, two men carrying guns were screaming at them through the window. As Bob Green drove away quickly, he could hear gunshots.

那時是傍晚。他們的孩子在後座睡著了。突然有兩個男人帶著槍透過窗戶對他們叫喊著。當 Bob Green 急駛離開，他聽到有槍聲。

❸ To escape my problems, I continued to turn to alcohol. I would spend every night in some dark, cheap bar drinking until early morning. I would stagger home to sleep until I awoke to begin the same routine again the next day.

（摘錄自 Edgar Allan Poe 的 *The Black Cat*）

為了逃避我的問題，我持續求助於酒精。我每晚都在廉價又黑暗的小酒吧喝到凌晨。我

蹣跚地晃回家睡直到醒來又繼續我另一天重複的生活。

④ As I answered an email from an online dating site, I got to thinking about the similarities between searching for someone to date and looking for a job. In both cases, your resume, profile and initial letter are the only thing standing between a dream life and rejection. (摘錄自 Reader's Digest by Meaghan Cameron's)

當我回信給一個交友網站時,我想到找個人約會跟找個工作之間的相似性。對於這兩件事,你的履歷、個人資料、和你說的第一個字都是那個決定你有美好人生或是被拒絕的唯一因素。

⑤ During Christine's childhood, her father tells her many stories featuring an "Angel of Music", who, like a muse, is the personification of musical inspiration. On his deathbed, Christine's father tells her that from Heaven, he will send the Angel of Music to her. (摘錄自 Answers.com)

在 Christine 的童年時期,她父親告訴她許多 "音樂天使" 的故事。音樂天使像是個繆斯女神,是啟發音樂靈感的化身。在他死前,他告訴她他會從天堂送一個音樂天使給她。

⑥ A man is speaking to a long-distance telephone operator.
"Could you please tell me the time difference between Taipei and Las Vegas?" asks the man.
"Just a minute", says the operator.
The man says "Thank you" and puts down the phone.
(摘錄自 www.rdasia.com)

一位男士正和長途電話接線員說話。「你可以告訴我台北跟賭城之間的時差是多久嗎?」男子問。接線生說:「一下下。」男子說:「喔!謝謝你。」然後就掛電話了。(Just a minute. 字面上翻譯成「只要一分鐘」,但實際上意義為「等一下下」)

⑦ You could predict the weather yourself. Just using nature as a forecast, you could easily predict what weather was coming. There are many ways to do this. Leeches, the moon, and even crickets can help. Clouds are one of the easiest clues to future weather. (改寫自 wikiHow.com)

你可以自己預測天氣。只要用大自然的線索來做預測,你可以輕易預測天氣將會如何。有許多方式可以這麼做。水蛭、月亮、甚至蟋蟀都有幫助,而雲朵是最容易預測天氣的線索之一。

⑧ Once upon a time as a queen sits sewing at her window, she pricks her finger on her needle and three drops of blood fall on the snow that had fallen on her ebony window frame. As she looks at the blood on the snow, she says to herself, "Oh, how I wish that I had a daughter that had skin white as snow, lips red as blood, and hair black as ebony". Soon after that, the queen gives birth to a baby girl who has skin white as snow, lips red as blood, and hair black as ebony. They name her Princess Snow White. （摘錄自 http://builders. forumotion.net/t883-snow-white-the-seven-dwarfs）

從前從前，有一個皇后坐在窗前縫紉，她不小心將針刺到手指，三滴鮮血滴落在黑檀木窗櫺上的白雪上。她對自己說：「喔！多希望我有一個皮膚白的像雪，嘴唇紅如鮮血，頭髮如檀木般漆黑的女兒。」之後不久，皇后生了一個女嬰，她的皮膚像雪一樣白，嘴唇像血一樣紅，頭髮像檀木一樣黑。他們便叫她「白雪公主」。

⑨ Although he lives alone, Tom feels the presence of society surrounding him. The railroad rushes past the pond near his house, interrupting his daydreams and forcing him to think about the development of technology. He also finds occasions to communicate with other people, such as the farmers, railroad workers, or some odd visitors.

雖然他獨居，Tom 仍感受到社會的存在並圍繞著他。鐵路火車在他屋子旁的湖邊疾駛而過，打斷了他做白日夢並迫使他去思考科技的發展。他也找到能和其他人溝通的機會，例如和農夫、鐵路工人、或一些奇怪的訪客。

⑩ While my friend Amy was visiting her mother, they went for a walk and bumped into an old family acquaintance. "Is this your daughter?" the woman asked. "Oh, I remember her when she was this high. How old is she now?" Without pausing, Amy's mother said, "Twenty-four." Amy, 35, nearly fainted on the spot. After everyone had said their good-byes, Amy asked her mother why she'd told such a whopper. "Well," she replied, "I've been lying about my age for so long, so I have to lie about yours too." （改寫自 www.rdasia.com: jokes）

當我朋友 Amy 去探望她的媽媽，她們去散步並遇見了一個老朋友。那女人問：「這是你女兒嗎？哇！我記得她那時才這麼高！現在她幾歲了？」毫不遲疑地，Amy 媽媽說：「24。」Amy，實際上 35 歲，差點當場昏倒。在每個人互道再會後，Amy 問媽媽為何撒這麼大的謊。她回答：「嗯……我長久以來都謊報我的年齡，所以我也必須要對你的年齡撒謊。」

❶（重點式）

Anderson Cooper, at the scene, get the story, find the truth, firsthand, AC 360, watch this reporter, get it right, coming up next, on CNN.（CNN 電視廣告）

Anderson Cooper，在現場，發現故事、找到真相、第一手資訊，AC360，看這個記者，得到正確的資訊，接下來登場，在 CNN 台。

❷（重點式）

Let's go.

It's the cleanest-burning fossil fuel. Shell is helping to deliver natural gas to more countries than any other energy company. We're trying to build a better energy future. Let's go. Shell.（摘錄自 www.shell.us/ naturalgas）

我們走！它是最乾淨可燃的化石燃料。Shell 比其他能源公司幫助傳送天然氣予更多國家。我們嘗試建立更好的能源未來。我們走！Shell。

☑fossil fuel（n.）化石燃料

❸（重點式）

Do you find yourself constantly sneezing and suffering from watery eyes? Stop suffering and try Anti-allergy! Our new capsule has been proven more effective than any other medicine on the market in suppressing allergy symptoms. Take one and feel free all day!

你有發現你自己持續打噴嚏和流眼淚嗎？不要再受苦了！試試 Anti-allergy！我們的新膠囊已證實了它比其他任何在市場上用來抑制過敏症狀的藥物都還有效。 服用一顆就能舒服一整天！

☑capsule（n.）膠囊　☑suppressing（v.）鎮壓、平定　☑allergy（n.）過敏

❹（重點式）

Are you looking to buy a used car? Come to Pretty Joe's Car Emporium. We have cars in every shape and size. The 2005 sedans are just $7,000, and 2008 minivans are only $8,000! Bad credit? No problem! We'll help you to drive home happily.

你要買台二手車嗎？來 Pretty Joe 的汽車百貨商店吧！我們有種類型大小的車，有 2005 年的轎車只要 7,000 元，2008 年的小型休旅車只要 8,000 元。沒有良好信用沒關係，我們會幫助你開心地把車開回家！

☑emporium（n.）大百貨店　☑sedans（n.）轎車

⑤（鋪陳式）

We're all about helping people. Helping them achieve their greatest dreams. Whether they're buying, selling, or renting, we help make it possible. We're about building communities, expanding businesses, creating a future, knowing what people value most, putting smiles on people's faces. We're about making careers, providing opportunities, opening doors, helping people reach their full potential. In every corner of the country, we help people find their perfect home. First National Real Estate: we put people first. （改寫自 First national Real Estate 廣告）

我們都在幫助人。幫助人們達成夢想，不管他們是要買、賣或租，我們幫助這些成為可能。我們建立社區、拓展事業、創造未來、知道人們最重視什麼、替人們臉上掛上笑容。我們製造工作、提供機會、敞開大門、幫助人們發揮潛能。在全國各地，我們幫助人們找到完美的家庭。第一國家不動產，我們視幫助人們為優先。

⑥（重點式）

Make the ultimate upgrade. To a Mac. Why get a new PC and just upgrade your computer, when you can get a Mac and upgrade your entire computer experience? A Mac is as good as it looks. From the outside in, a Mac is designed to be a better computer. Try Mac. Choose Mac. And you will love Mac. （摘錄自 http://www.apple.com/why-mac/）

極致升級，Mac。為何要買一台 PC 只升級你的電腦而不買一台 Mac 來升級你使用電腦的全部經驗？Mac 跟他的外表一樣優秀。從裡到外，Mac 是被設計為一種更好的電腦。試試 Mac，選擇 Mac，你會愛上 Mac。

⑦（重點式）

There comes a time, when you reach a new chapter in your life, when your body's changed, and your knees have changed, that's why there's Centrum Silver, the complete multi-vitamin especially for adults 50 and up. To help support immunity, vitality, and overall good health, for this chapter in your life, embrace life's changes with Centrum Silver. （改寫自 Centrum Silver 電視廣告）

時間到了，當你開啟了人生的另一頁，當你的身體改變了，你的膝蓋也變了，這就是 Centrum Silver 存在的原因。包含多種維他命，特別針對 50 歲以上，來幫助支持免疫力、生命力以及良好的健康。為了你生命的這一頁，讓 Centrum Silver 陪你一起擁抱生命的改變。

☑multi-vitamin（*n.*）多種維他命　☑immunity（*n.*）免疫力　☑vitality（*n.*）活力

☑embrace (v.) 擁抱

Lesson 12 參考解答與翻譯

① clouds / rain / north / east / clouds / rain / southern
② windy / rainy / typhoon / 20-24
③ sunny / rain / showers / 20 / north / 22 / east / 21 / south
④ clear / sunny / cold / dropping / 5 / Tomorrow / Friday / sunny / cloudy / eastern / weekend / 40
⑤ sunshine / front / 70% / chance / of / rain / 15 / below / 10 / 0 / Wednesday / morning / low / 20s
⑥ sunny / windy / high-pressure / 75 / miles / Warnings
⑦ winter / storm / warning / cold / front / blizzard / evening / blackouts

【參考翻譯】
① 今明兩天的台灣天氣預報是多雲以及短暫雨在北部以及東部。中部以及南部多雲但不會下雨。
② Ferilla 也是有風有雨的天氣。該地區的美麗海灘因為颱風而關閉。想去那邊度假的旅客將必須改變計畫。今天該城市的氣溫是攝氏 20-24 度。
③ 今天是晴天。下了一個星期的雨，太陽終於出來了。來看一下現在的氣溫，北部 20 度以上，島嶼中部 22 度，東部以及南部地區 21 度。
④ 今天的天氣將會是個晴朗的太陽天，但晚上會變冷，氣溫也會掉到 5 度以下。明天以及星期五大部分是晴天但部分東部山區會是陰天。周末時，南風會將高溫推到近 40 度。
⑤ 現在是氣象報告時間，在享受了這幾天的陽光之後，你可能要失望了。明天將有一道冷鋒面來襲並會造成 70% 的降雨機率，氣溫也會降到攝氏 15 度左右。凌晨溫度會降到 10 度以下，部分地區可能還會接近 0 度。但別擔心，情況到星期三早上會好轉，最低氣溫 20 度，週末會晴朗。
⑥ 今天的天氣跟昨天一樣晴朗，但明天以及後天會變得有風。有一個高氣壓從南邊移上來，我們預計會有每小時高達 75 英哩的強風來襲。針對在路上的駕駛和工作者發出警報。
⑦ 氣象局發部冬日暴雨警報。今天晚上，冷鋒將會給南加州山區帶來暴風雪。當地居民要有停電準備，而遊客應該要延後行程。

Lesson 13 參考解答與翻譯

① The suspect in a bombing and mass shooting that happened in Norway on Friday has acknowledged carrying out the attacks to combat what he claimed to be the "colonization" of Norway by Muslims, a judge said last Monday. （改寫自 http://edition.cnn.com/）

一位法官上星期一表示，上個月在波蘭發生的爆炸及大眾槍擊事件的嫌疑犯承認他做出這些攻擊行動是為了反對回教徒在波蘭的殖民。

☑acknowledge（*v.*）承認　☑combat（*v.*）反對　☑colonization（*n.*）殖民
☑Muslim（*n.*）回教徒　☑judge（*n.*）法官

❷ A bullet train was struck from behind by another train in southeastern China, killing at least 38 people, including two American citizens, and injuring almost 200. The first train was forced to stop on the tracks due to a power outage and the impact caused six cars to derail, including four that fell from an elevated bridge. （摘錄自 The Coming Crisis. blogspot.com.）

中國東南方一輛高速鐵路火車被後方另一輛火車追撞事件，造成至少 38 人死亡，其中包括兩名美國公民，以及近 200 人受傷。第一輛火車因為電力不足而被迫停在軌道上，撞擊的衝力使得六輛車廂出軌，其中有四輛掉落高架橋下。

☑bullet train（*n.*）高速火車　☑elevated bridge（*n.*）高架橋

❸ Last week, Serena Williams, 29, the famous tennis player, told the world that she is back. She took just 47 minutes to defeat the Russian player Maria Sharapora in only her third tournament back after nearly a year out of the sport following two foot operations and a blood clot in her lung. "I wanted to be more consistent, and I think I did that tonight," the American told a post-match press conference. （改寫自 http://edition.cnn.com/）

上星期，29 歲的網球好手 Serena Williams 告訴全世界的每個人，她回來了。她只花了 47 分鐘便擊敗了俄國選手 Maria Sharapora。這只是她離開接近一年去接受兩次腳部手術與一次肺部血塊移除後的第三場比賽。這位美國人在賽後記者招待會上說：「我要像以前一樣，而我想我今晚做到了。」

☑tournament（*n.*）比賽　☑consistent（*adj.*）始終如一的

❹ Today, the legislature passed a new federal law requiring companies to offer all their employees, including part-time workers, health insurance. Lawmakers believe that this will reduce workers' financial burden. Though most businesses believe the law will not have much effect on their everyday operations or overall finances, many employees fear that their salary may be slashed. The new law will come into effect from March 1st next year, and will affect more than 50,000 workers.

今天，立法機關通過了一項新的聯邦法條要求公司必須提供給包括臨時工等全部員工們健康保險。立法者相信這將會減低員工的財務負擔。雖然大多數公司行號相信這條法律不影響他們的每日運作與整體經濟，但許多員工們害怕他們的薪水將會被砍低。這項新法將會於明年三月一日實施，並會影響超過 50,000 位員工。

☑legislature（*n.*）立法機構　☑slash（*v.*）猛砍

⑤ **Russell Crowe might play Jor-El in the new Superman movie**

The producers of 1978's "Superman: The Movie" hired Marlon Brando, an Oscar-winning actor, to play Superman's father Jor-El. The latest news is that this role might be acted by another Oscar-winner Russell Crowe. According to variety, Crowe is currently in talks to play Jor-El in "Man of Steel" next year. Warner Bros., producer Christopher Nolan, and director Zack Snyder had no comment on the casting news, but it's worth exploring what the news might mean for the movie.（改寫自 EW.com）

Russell Crowe 可能在新的超人電影中扮演 Jor-El

1978 年 "超人：電影" 的製片聘請了奧斯卡最佳男演員得主 Marlon Brando 飾演超人的父親 Jor-El。最新消息是這個角色可能會被另一位奧斯卡得主 Russell Crowe 飾演。根據 variety 雜誌，Crowe 正在談明年在 "Man of Steel" 這部電影中飾演 Jor-El。華納兄弟公司的製片 Christopher Nolan 和導演 Zack Snyder 對演出名單新聞不予置評，但探討這個新聞對這部電影有什麼意義是很有價值的。

☑casting（*n.*）角色分派

Lesson 14 　參考解答與翻譯

❶（運動比賽）

A: The Lions beat the Bears.

B: But I thought the Bears were leading the whole game.

A: Yeah, but the Lions scored with two seconds left to win by a point.

A：獅隊已經打敗熊隊了。

B：但我認為在整場比賽中，一直都是由熊隊領先著。

A：是啊！但在比賽結束前兩秒獅隊得分，結果以一分險勝對方。

❷（餐廳）

Good evening, and welcome to Tommy Ribs. Our special tonight is the cheese lobster and sirloin steak. It comes with our famous chef salad made with fresh romaine lettuce and also a soft drink. Today's dessert is apple pie or chocolate ice cream. Here are the menus and I'll be back in a few moments to take your order.

晚安，歡迎來到 Tommy Ribs。我們今晚的特餐是起司龍蝦和沙朗牛排，搭配我們知名的主廚沙拉，是用新鮮蘿蔓生菜做的，還有一杯飲料。甜點是蘋果派或巧克力冰淇淋。菜單在這，我過一會兒再來為你們點餐。

❸（商店）

A: Excuse me. I purchased this suitcase last month, but the first time I tried to use it, the handle came off. I want to exchange it for a new one.

B: I'm really sorry about that. Let me see what I can do for you. Do you have your receipt?

A: No, I don't have it with me.

B: Umm ... I am sure that we can exchange it for a new one, but we need to see your receipt first. That's our company policy. I hope you understand.

A：不好意思打擾一下，我上個月買了這個手提箱，但我第一次用它，把手就掉了，我想要換個新的。

B：我真的感到很抱歉，讓我看看我能為你做什麼。請問你有帶你的收據嗎？

A：沒有，我沒有帶在身上。

B：嗯……我很確定我們可以換一個新的給你，但我們必須先看到你的收據。這是公司的規定，希望你能理解。

❹（商店）

A: I was here two days ago and purchased these shoes, but they are too big. I'd like to return them.

B: I remember you. You came here in the afternoon. I'm sorry we only allow exchanges.

A: I see. But you don't have a smaller size, right? Or I wouldn't have bought size 7 at that time.

B: Let me call our downtown location and see if they have any in stock.

A：我兩天前才在這裡買了這雙鞋，但太大了，我想要退貨。

B：我記得你，你是下午來的。我很抱歉我們只能接受換貨。

A：好吧！但你們沒有小一點的尺寸，對吧？ 要不然我那時也不會買 7 號。

B：讓我打電話問問市區分店看看他們有沒有存貨。

❶ 391 / Taichung / 9:15

❷ fog / tomorrow / delayed / website / two

❸ turbulence / return / fasten / turned / off / overhead / under / sickness / bag / button / on / your / armrest

❹ KMS / Airline / flight / 273 / 9:45 / Paris / blizzard / transfer / 30

❺ Checking / in / reservation / Lucy / Wang / single / three / sign

【參考翻譯】

❶ 各位旅客請注意，9 點 15 分開往台中的第 391 次列車即將進站，搭乘本列車的旅客，請前往月台候車，上車時請留意月台間隙。祝您旅途愉快！

　　✓ bound（*adj.*）正在前往的、打算去的　✓ proceed（*v.*）繼續前進

　　✓ board（*v.*）搭上（船、飛機、車）

❷ A：丹佛機場你好，早安。

　　B：我看到新聞說丹佛機場附近有霧，我擔心我明天的班機。起飛時刻表將會變更，對嗎？

　　A：是的，沒錯。因為能見度很差所以所有班機都延後了，我們希望明天中午霧會散開。關於新的時刻表，你可以在出發前上我們的網站查詢。我們每兩小時會更新班機行程一次。

　　B：好，我會在網站上查詢，謝謝。

　　A：不客氣，感謝你打來。

　　✓ visibility（*n.*）能見度

❸ 晚安各位先生女士，我是你們的機長。幾分鐘後我們會進入到強烈亂流的區域。請回座位並繫上安全帶，請留在座位上直到繫安全帶的顯示燈熄滅為止。也請確認你的包包已妥善地收在頭上的行李櫃或是放置在你前面的座位底下。如果你需要嘔吐袋，它在你前方的袋子裡。如果你有任何疑問或需要任何事物，請按下你扶手上的按鈕以聯絡我們的空服人員。

　　✓ turbulence（*n.*）亂流　✓ fasten（*v.*）繫緊、栓緊　✓ compartment（*n.*）隔間

　　✓ pouch（*n.*）小袋　✓ armrest（*n.*）扶手

❹ 請注意。很抱歉要通知您 KMS 航空原訂 9:45 要飛往巴黎的第 273 班機因為暴風雪而延遲了。所有要搭乘該航班的旅客必須要稍等之後進一步的消息。如果你有和關於延遲或轉機的問題，請聯絡位在 30 號登機門的顧客服務部櫃台。

❺ A：午安。要入住房間嗎？

　　B：是。

A：有訂房嗎？

B：有。我訂過了，我的名字是 Lucy Wang。

A：歡迎！讓我看看單子……在這裏。你需要一間單人房住 3 天。對嗎？

B：是的。

A：請填寫住宿登記表，並請在這裡簽名。

Lesson 16　參考解答與翻譯

① nonstop / Vancouver / no / seats / available / economy / business / next / six / the / next / vegetarian / meal / next / flight

② half / an / hour / ago / cellphone / table / my / seat / front / area / piano / 910-3490

③ busy / stay / 9 / your / name / phone / number / main / menu / 0

④ Lion / Bank / loan / balance / 2 / late / payment / 3 / 9

⑤ Ruby / high / school / classmate / wrong / tenant / two / months

【參考翻譯】

① A：是 TS 航空嗎？我是 Terry Sheldon，打電話來確認我訂的溫哥華直飛班機。

　　B：好的，Sheldon 先生。我們有接到您的訂位，但很抱歉沒有經濟艙的位子了。我幫您訂了一個商務艙的位子，或是您也可以搭乘晚六小時的下一個班次。

　　A：這樣啊！那我訂下一個班次好了，還有，別忘了我訂了素食餐。

　　B：現在幫您預訂了下一個航班，也在上面註記您的特餐。

② A：嗨！我是 Kevin Morris，我半小時前離開你們餐廳然後我現在找不到我的手機。可以請你幫我確認一下它是否有掉在我座位嗎？我坐在前方，鋼琴的附近。

　　B：沒問題，Morris 先生。我會叫我們的員工立刻幫您檢查。這可能需要一點時間，有沒有其他方式我們可以連絡您？

　　A：真的非常謝謝你的幫助。請打我太太的電話 910-3490。

　　B：先生請別擔心。我相信它會出現的。

③ 這裡是 Wix 電腦產品支援部。所有的分機都在忙線中，如果你在線上，我們會盡快為您服務。如果你無法等待並希望我們回你電話，請按 9 並錄下你的名字、電話、和技術問題。如果要回到主選單，請按 0。我們感謝你的耐心。

④ 感謝您打電話到獅子銀行。詢問貸款額度，請按 1。辦理自動扣款，請按 2。辦理延遲繳款，請按 3。如果你想要詢問貸款服務員其他問題，請按 9。

⑤ A：嗨，Ruby。我是 Ronny，你的高中同學。

　　B：嗯……恐怕你是打錯電話了。

　　A：喔！抱歉！你認識 Ruby Shelly 嗎？

解答篇

B：不，我不認識。她可能是上一個房客。我兩個月前才搬進來的。

A：這樣啊！再次抱歉，打擾你了。

❶ 目的：to celebrate and appreciate for the achievement, there is a company picnic

活動舉辦的時間 / 地點：on Saturday / in Memorial Park

錄音內容與翻譯

Thanks for coming to our staff meeting today. It is with great pride that I announce that our mobile telephone coverage area has grown. I know that you have all worked very hard and I want to thank you for your great efforts. To celebrate our achievement, and to show you our appreciation, we will be having a company picnic in Memorial Park on Saturday. Your families are welcome to join us. I hope you can all come to the picnic.

感謝員工們來參加今天的會議。我非常驕傲地公佈我們手機分佈的範圍又增加了。我知道你們都工作很努力也謝謝你們的付出。為了慶祝我們的成就也為了表示對你們的感謝，我們將於星期六在紀念公園舉辦一場公司野餐會。歡迎大家的家人們也一同參與，希望你們全部都能來。

❷ 目的：to plan a good-bye party for the CEO, Mr. Woods

活動舉辦的時間：September 20th

錄音內容與翻譯

We're here today to plan a good-bye party for our CEO, Mr. Woods. He's going to retire next month, and I think it is necessary to hold a party for him. He's worked for our company for 20 years, since he was 39, and he's also taught us many things. The party is set for September 20th. It's a Friday, and also his last day working here. We'll have two weeks to arrange it, but let's start now. We have an hour before he finishes his meeting on the tenth floor. Quick! Who has any ideas?

今天，我們聚在這裡是為了要替我們的 CEO（Chief Executive Officer 首席執行長）Woods 先生設計一個餞別會。他即將於下個月退休，我認為替他辦一個派對是一定要的。他自 39 歲起，為我們公司工作已經 20 年了，他也教了我們很多事。派對在 9 月 20 日舉行，那是個星期五，也是他在這工作的最後一天。我們有 2 個星期來籌備，現在就開始吧。他在 10 樓開完會之前，我們還有一個小時可以討論。快！誰有任何想法？

❸ 建議一：kidnapping him and take him to the beach

是否被接受 / 原因：X. The headquarters will not allow.

建議二：<u>making a video for him</u>

是否被接受／原因：○. It is touching.

录音内容与翻译

A: Do we have to work on that day? I remember he likes the beach. Maybe we can kidnap him and take him to the beach.

B: What a crazy idea! I like it, but I don't think the headquarters will allow us to do that. Any other ideas?

C: Maybe we can make a video for him, and play it at the party. We can collect some pictures and also record everyone's messages to Mr. Woods.

B: Yeah! Good idea! Let's make a documentary about his time at the company. How touching!

A: I like it, too.

B: So you are responsible for collecting the pictures, Molly; and you for the filming, Watson, because you have the camera. I'll email all of you about the details of the plan. Remember, don't tell him anything about this party. It's top secret.

A：我們那天要上班嗎？我記得他喜歡海邊，或許我們可以綁架他到海邊。

B：多麼瘋狂的主意！我喜歡！但我不認為總公司會讓我們這麼做。有沒有其他想法？

C：或許我們可以為他做一段影片，然後在派對時播放。我們可以收集一些他的照片，也可以錄每個人給 woods 先生的一段話。

B：對啊！真棒的想法！我們幫他做他在公司的紀錄。多感人啊！

A：我也喜歡這個想法。

B：那麼，Molly，你去負責收集照片。Watson 你負責錄影，因為你有攝影機。我會用電子郵件寄細節給你們全部的人。記住，千萬不可以讓他知道關於派對的任何事，這是最高機密。

✓headquarter（*n.*）總部

Lesson 18　參考解答與翻譯

❶ 答案：A

題目與選項翻譯

車諾比核電廠。

這段講的主題是什麼？

A：Pripyat 居民所受的影響／ B：輻射汙染的嚴重性／ C：爆炸的原因

錄音內容與翻譯

On April 26, 1986, Reactor 4 at the Chernobyl Nuclear Power Plant near the town of Pripyat, Ukraine, exploded. The explosion took place at 1:23 a.m. while the neighboring town of Pripyat slept. Two workers were killed instantly. Forty hours later, the residents of Pripyat were ordered to evacuate, and most never returned; by that time, many of the residents had suffered varying degrees of radiation poisoning. （摘錄自 Zomoco "Chernobyl Disaster"）

1986 年 4 月 26 日，烏克蘭的 Pripyat 鎮旁的車諾比核電廠第 4 反應爐爆炸了。發生的時間是凌晨 1:23，當時鄰近的 Pripyat 居民都正在睡夢中。2 名員工立即死亡，40 個小時後，Pripyat 的居民井然有序地被安排撤離，而且大部分的人就都沒有回去了。自那時候開始，許多居民便承受著不同程度輻射汙染的折磨。

☑ reactor（n.）核能反應爐　☑ Ukraine（n.）烏克蘭　☑ evacuate（v.）撤離、撤退
☑ radiation（n.）輻射線

❷ 答案：A
題目與選項翻譯

出生排序。

哪一句是正確的論點？ A：有許多人不相信出生排序這個理論 / B：排行老大的孩子較為社交化並善於協商 / C：出生排序會影響那個人未來工作的好壞

錄音內容與翻譯

There is a theory that a person's place in a family's birth order can have a powerful effect on one's personality. It determines how you feel, how you behave, and it affects your relationships. It affects the mate that you choose to marry and the job that you choose to do. The first child, most of the time, is self-confident. The middle child is more social and good at negotiation. And the youngest child is charming, but overly humble. These statements seem convincing, but there are still many scholars who disagree with the theory.

有一派理論相信一個人在家庭中的排行對個性有很大的影響，它決定了你怎麼感受、怎麼做出行為以及你的人際關係。它也對你選擇結婚對象與工作有影響。排行第一的孩子絕大部分的時候是很有自信的，排在中間的小孩比較具有社交跟溝通的能力，而最小的孩子很有魅力但太過謙卑。雖然這些論點很有說服力，但仍有許多學者懷疑這個理論。

☑ determine（v.）決定　☑ negotiation（n.）談判、協商　☑ scholar（n.）學者

❸ 答案：C
題目與選項翻譯

心理學。

哪一句是正確的論點？ A：心理學的目標是要了解人類的發展 / B：心理學家研究人的

心理疾病／ C：心理學是一門科學

Many people might be curious about what psychology is? What do psychologists do? Psychology is the science of behavior and mental processes. Its goal is to understand individuals and groups by both establishing general principles and researching specific cases. However, the ultimate goal of psychology is to benefit society. In this field, a professional practitioner or researcher is called a psychologist, and can be classified as a social scientist, behavioral scientist, or cognitive scientist.（改寫自 Wikipedia, "psychology"）

許多人或許會對心理學到底是什麼而感到好奇，而心理學家到底是做什麼的？新理學是一門關於研究心理與行為之間過程的科學。它的目標是要藉由建立普遍原則和研究個別案件來了解個人與團體；而心理學的終極目標是要為社會謀福利。在這個領域裡，專業從事人員或研究者被稱為心理學家，他是可以被歸類於社會科學家、行為科學家、或認知科學家。

⊘ cognitive（*adj.*）認知的

❹ 答案：B

科幻小說。

哪一句是正確的論點？ A：科幻小說是關於過去與我們的世界／ B：讀者可能會以為故事中的一些事是真實的／ C：Steven King 不止是科學家也是科幻小說家

Science fiction is literary prose written with a scientific theme. It is about the future, space, other worlds, etc. These stories usually have some basis in scientific fact, so readers will feel that such things could be real. Many of America's early science fiction stories were published in magazines. *Amazing Stories*, begun in 1926, was the first magazine devoted to this kind of literature. Steven King and Ray Bradbury are the most popular science fiction writers today. Issac Asimov was a scientist as well as a science fiction writer.

科幻小說是一種以科學為主題的文學性散文，它關於著未來、太空或其他世界等等。這些故事通常有科學的基礎事實，所以讀者會覺得有些東西是真實的。許多美國早期科幻小說是在雜誌上發表，1926 年開始的 Amazing Stories（驚奇故事）雜誌就是最早致力於這類型文學的雜誌。Steven King 和 Ray Bradbury 是現今最有名的科幻小說家之一，

解答篇

而 Issac Asimov 是科學家也同時是科幻小說家。

☑literary（*adj.*）文學的　☑prose（*n.*）散文　☑theme（*n.*）主題

Lesson 19 參考解答與翻譯

❶ Dreaming is universal.

題目與選項翻譯

這段話中你覺得主要的重點是什麼？

錄音內容與翻譯

Connie, a 5-year-old girl, dreams of her teddy bear every night. Her grandmother, 85 years old, sleeps 18 hours a day, and dreams about her hometown all the time. Dreaming is universal. It unites all people across boundaries of age, sex, race and religion. Dreams are the doorways to spiritual experiences for everyone.（改寫自 Discovery video, "The Power of Dream"）

Connie，一個五歲的女孩，每天晚上都會夢到她的泰迪熊。她 85 歲的奶奶每天睡 18 個小時，總是在夢中夢到她的家鄉。夢是普遍的，不論何種年紀、性別、種族或宗教，夢境統一了全部的人。夢境是每個人通往精神經驗的入口。

☑boundary（*n.*）邊界　☑doorway（*n.*）出入口　☑spiritual（*adj.*）精神上的

❷（1）There are many shopping malls and amusement parks for adults and children.

（2）There are many modern and postmodern buildings in the downtown area.

（3）There are plenty of natural spaces.

（4）You can have an adventure to southern China by railway.

題目與選項翻譯

根據這個節目，為何香港是亞洲最棒的旅遊地點？

錄音內容與翻譯

Where is the best travel destination in Asia? Today we'll be talking about the best destination for both city lovers and nature lovers. The place is Hong Kong. There are many shopping malls and amusement parks for adults and children. There are many modern and postmodern buildings in the downtown area. In the north of Hong Kong and the area near the airport, there are plenty of natural spaces. With your passport, you can even have an adventure to southern China by railway from Hong Kong.

亞洲最棒的旅遊地點在哪？今天，我們將來談談哪個地點對城市愛好者和大自然愛好者都是最棒的。那裡就是香港。香港有很多購物中心跟遊樂場適合成人與小孩。在市中心有很多現代和後現代的建築。在香港北部與機場附近區域也有很多自然風景。帶著你的護照，你甚至可以從香港搭鐵路去南中國探險。

☑amusement park（*n.*）遊樂園　☑postmodern（*adj.*）後現代

③ B

題目與選項翻譯

這段話的重點是什麼？ A：這個男子跟這個女子求婚。 / B：Joey 跟這個女子求婚。 / C：這個女子要訂婚了。

錄音內容與翻譯

Man: I heard about your engagement.

Woman: Surprised?

Man: … And confused! … I didn't propose to you.

Woman: I know.

Man: I don't think you do.

Woman: You didn't propose to me. Joey did.

（摘錄自 Friends 影集）

男：我聽說你訂婚的事了。

女：驚訝嗎？

男：恩……很困惑！ 我沒有跟你求婚！

女：我知道。

男：我不認為你知道。

女：你沒有跟我求婚，但是 Joey 有。

④ B

題目與選項翻譯

那個男子有 "諷刺" 的牌子？ A：是的，他有。 / B：不，這也是諷刺。 / C：也許，我們不知道。

錄音內容與翻譯

A: Good morning.

B: Good morning.

A: I have to say I slept splendidly. Granted, not long, but just deeply and well.

B: I'm not surprised. A well-known folk cure for insomnia is to break in to your neighbor's apartment and clean it.

A: Sarcasm?

B: You think?

A: Granted, my methods may have been somewhat unusual, but I think the end result will be a measurable enhancement to her quality of life.

B: You've convinced me. Maybe tonight we should sneak in and shampoo her carpet.

A: Don't you think that crosses a line?

B: Yes. For god's sake! Do I have to hold up a sarcasm sign every time I open my month?

A: You have a sarcasm sign?

(quoted from "The Big Theory" season 1:2)

A：早！

B：早！

A：我必須要說我睡的非常香甜。雖然時間不長但是睡眠品質很好。

B：我不感到驚訝，傳說中的治失眠靈藥就是闖到鄰居家裡打掃。

A：諷刺？

B：你覺得呢？

A：就算是吧！我的方法可能有點唐突，但是我認為這是提高她的生活品質很好的方式。

B：你說的對。也許今晚我們應該偷偷溜進去把她的地毯洗了。

A：你不覺得那太過分了嗎？

B：對!!!!! 天啊!!!!! 每次我開口說話都得舉著 "諷刺" 的牌子嗎？

A：你有寫 "諷刺" 的牌子？

☑ splendidly（*adv.*）壯麗地　☑ granted（*con.*）就算　☑ insomnia（*n.*）失眠

☑ sarcasm（*n.*）諷刺　☑ measurable（*adj.*）可測量的

☑ enhancement（*n.*）提高、增加　☑ sneak（*v.*）偷溜

國家圖書館出版品預行編目資料

改變一生的英文聽力課 / 陳超明作. -- 初版. -- 臺北市;
貝塔出版 : 智勝文化發行, 2012. 1
　　面： 　公分

　ISBN: 978-957-729-863-8（平裝附光碟）

　1. 英語　2. 讀本

805.18　　　　　　　　　　　　　　　　100022078

改變一生的英文聽力課

作　　者 / 陳超明
整　　理 / 黃郁雯
執行編輯 / 朱慧瑛

出　　版 / 貝塔出版有限公司
地　　址 / 台北市 100 館前路 12 號 11 樓
電　　話 / (02) 2314-2525
傳　　真 / (02) 2312-3535
郵　　撥 / 19493777 貝塔出版有限公司
客服專線 / (02) 2314-3535
客服信箱 / btservice@betamedia.com.tw

總 經 銷 / 時報文化出版企業股份有限公司
地　　址 / 桃園縣龜山鄉萬壽路二段 351 號
電　　話 / (02) 2306-6842

出版日期 / 2012 年 11 月初版五刷
定　　價 / 350 元
I S B N / 978-957-729-863-8

改變一生的英文聽力課
Copyright 2012 by 陳超明
Published by Beta Multimedia Publishing

貝塔網址：www.betamedia.com.tw

喚醒你的英文語感 ！

請對折後釘好，直接寄回即可！

廣　告　回　信
北區郵政管理局登記證
北 台 字 第 1 4 2 5 6 號
免　貼　郵　票

100 台北市中正區館前路12號11樓

貝塔語言出版 收
Beta Multimedia Publishing

寄件者住址

貝塔語言出版
Beta Multimedia Publishing

讀者服務專線 (02) 2314-3535　讀者服務傳真 (02) 2312-3535
客戶服務信箱 btservice@betamedia.com.tw
www.betamedia.com.tw

謝謝您購買本書！！

貝塔語言擁有最優良之英文學習書籍，為提供您最佳的英語學習資訊，您填妥此表後寄回（免貼郵票），將可不定期免費收到本公司最新發行之書訊及活動訊息！

姓名：＿＿＿＿＿＿＿＿　性別：☐男 ☐女　生日：＿＿年＿＿月＿＿日

電話：（公）＿＿＿＿＿＿（宅）＿＿＿＿＿＿＿（手機）＿＿＿＿＿＿

電子信箱：＿＿＿＿＿＿＿＿＿＿＿＿＿＿＿＿＿＿＿＿＿＿

學歷：☐高中職含以下　☐專科　☐大學　☐研究所含以上

職業：☐金融　☐服務　☐傳播　☐製造　☐資訊　☐軍公教　☐出版
　　　☐自由　☐教育　☐學生　☐其他

職級：☐企業負責人　☐高階主管　☐中階主管　☐職員　☐專業人士

1. 您購買的書籍是？＿＿＿＿＿＿＿＿＿＿＿＿＿＿＿＿

2. 您從何處得知本產品？（可複選）

　☐書店 ☐網路 ☐書展 ☐校園活動 ☐廣告信函 ☐他人推薦 ☐新聞報導 ☐其他＿＿

3. 您覺得本產品價格：

　☐偏高 ☐合理 ☐偏低

4. 請問目前您每週花了多少時間學英語？

　☐不到十分鐘 ☐十分鐘以上，但不到半小時 ☐半小時以上，但不到一小時
　☐一小時以上，但不到兩小時 ☐兩個小時以上 ☐不一定

5. 通常在選擇語言學習書時，哪些因素是您會考慮的？

　☐封面 ☐內容、實用性 ☐品牌 ☐媒體、朋友推薦 ☐價格 ☐其他＿＿

6. 市面上您最需要的語言書種類為？

　☐聽力 ☐閱讀 ☐文法 ☐口說 ☐寫作 ☐其他＿＿

7. 通常您會透過何種方式選購語言學習書籍？

　☐書店門市 ☐網路書店 ☐郵購 ☐直接找出版社 ☐學校或公司團購 ☐其他＿＿

8. 給我們的建議：＿＿＿＿＿＿＿＿＿＿＿＿＿＿＿＿

　＿＿＿＿＿＿＿＿＿＿＿＿＿＿＿＿＿＿＿＿＿＿

　＿＿＿＿＿＿＿＿＿＿＿＿＿＿＿＿＿＿＿＿＿＿

喚醒你的英文語感！

Get a Feel for English !

喚醒你的英文語感！

Get a Feel for English !